Prairie Schooner Book Prize in Fiction | EDITOR: Kwame Dawes

Now We Will Be Happy

Amina Gautier

UNIVERSITY OF NEBRASKA PRESS | LINCOLN AND LONDON

∞

This work was partially sup-
ported by a grant from the Illinois
Arts Council, a state agency.

Library of Congress
Cataloging-in-Publication Data
Gautier, Amina, 1977–
[Short stories. Selections]
Now we will be happy / Amina Gautier.
pages   cm.
— (Prairie Schooner Book Prize in Fiction)
ISBN 978-0-8032-5539-5 (pbk.: alk. paper)
ISBN 978-0-8032-5691-0 (epub)
ISBN 978-0-8032-5692-7 (mobi)
ISBN 978-0-8032-5690-3 (pdf)
I. Title.
PS3607.A976N69 2014
813'.6—dc23
2014010110

Set in Minion by L. Auten.
Designed by N. Putens.

Contents

Acknowledgments *vii*

Aguanile *1*

Now We Will Be Happy *16*

Bodega *28*

Muñeca *38*

How to Make Flan *53*

Only Son *67*

A Wish, Like a Candle, Burns *80*

The Luckiest Man in the World *93*

Remembering *98*

The Last Hurricane *114*

Palabras *119*

Acknowledgments

SOME OF THESE stories first appeared in *Chattahoochee Review*, *Crab Orchard Review*, *Glimmer Train Stories*, *Kenyon Review*, *Nimrod*, *Ocean State Review*, *Peralta Press*, *Salt Hill*, and *Southwest Review*. I wish to thank the editors of these magazines.

I also wish to express my gratitude to the Breadloaf Writer's Conference, Hurston/Wright Foundation, Illinois Arts Council, Prairie Center of the Arts, Sewanee Writer's Conference, and Writers in the Heartland. My thanks to Noreen Cargill, Michael Collier, Peter Covino, Kwame Dawes, Eleanor Jackson, Sheryl Johnston, Randall Kenan, David Lynn, Mike Levine, Rachel May, Erin McGraw, Robin Miura, Cherie Peters, Francine Ringold, Lydia Ship, Linda Swanson-Davies, Willard Spiegelman, Barbara and Wyatt Prunty, and Margherita Tortura.

Special thanks to Peter Rock, who read the very first story, and to Jon Tribble and Allison Joseph, who published it.

My thanks to my family: my mother, Sharon, my uncle Ricardo, my uncle Pete (Pedro), my cousin Stephen, and my titi Carmen y tio Cecil.

My thanks to mi familia: mi abuelo Pedro, mi abuela Olga, mi titi Tita, mi tio Roque, mi tio Petersito (Pedro), y mi titi Irma.

Most important of all, my thanks, my love, my gratitude, my reverence, my heart—all to Gloria Gautier, my Grammies, whose very life provoked the questions that I sought answers to through these stories.

¡Gracias por todo!

NOW WE WILL BE HAPPY

Aguanile

THE PHONE CALLS from my grandfather began after Charlie Palmieri died. Grief-stricken, my grandfather called each time one of his favorite musicians passed away. Delicately, he announced the passing as if it were that of a family member or someone we had actually known. The calls had little to do with any ability on my part to appreciate the musicians he revered. He turned to me by default; none of his children shared his interest in the music. My mother and uncles eschewed all things Puerto Rican, and his second set of children shunned his tastes, preferring hip-hop and Top 40 tunes. Though not the aficionado he was, I had spent my summer vacation humoring him, and now he treated me like a fellow enthusiast, viewing me as a sympathetic comrade, a person who shared his first family's blood but not its resentment.

The first call came on a weekday evening in mid-September. Summer wouldn't officially end for another week, but I had already started school. I was back in Brooklyn, completing my new junior high school homework at the kitchen table, when he called.

"Nena," he said. "I'm glad it's you. I have very bad news. Charlie has died."

"Uncle Chalí?"

"Charlie Palmieri," he said impatiently. "Remember I played 'Porque me Engañas' for you? That's his song."

"I'm sorry to hear that," I said, baffled by his ability to grieve for a stranger.

"Yes, me too," he said. "Such a surprise. A tragedy. Nobody could expect it."

Silence stretched between us, but my grandfather stayed on the line. So I asked, "How did he die?"

"The heart, nena," he said. "It was his poor heart."

In the living room, my grandmother, mother, and two uncles huddled around the TV watching news of Hurricane Gilbert, the tropical storm that had been whipping Jamaica for the past two days and was rumored to be headed our way in New York. I turned away from the footage of Gilbert's wreckage—destroyed crops, homes, buildings, and aircraft—to look down at my books open on the kitchen table, at my pencils next to the roll of paper towels and the canister of salt. "He's in a better place now. Better the next world than this one," I said, repeating words of comfort I'd once overheard my grandmother give.

There was an intake of breath on my grandfather's end. "So true," he said. "Thank you, nena."

"Do you want to speak to anyone?" I asked. "They're all here."

"Maybe another time," he said. Then he disconnected the call.

They had made a gift of me, sending me to him the summer I was twelve. Three days after my sixth-grade graduation, I'd boarded a plane for Puerto Rico, traveling with my grandfather's sister, Titi Inez. For me, it was a summer of firsts. I had never met my grandfather and I had never been on a plane. Between the two, meeting my grandfather frightened me most. The little I knew of flying had come from watching *Airplane!*, so I expected it would be all in good fun and—secretly—I hoped for a seat beside Kareem Abdul-Jabbar. My family tried to prepare me for the journey, but my mother and uncles had been on a plane only once themselves, flying as young children to make a similar trip across the Atlantic to see the father who had neither loved nor wanted them enough to stay.

I had hoped never to meet him. He was the husband my grand-mother had chosen not to remember, the father my mother and uncles refused to claim, the grandfather I knew only through pictures. I didn't want to spend a month of my summer with him, but I was to be a peace offering, an olive branch extended between families, sent across the ocean to knit back wounds whose ragged edges had grown frayed with each passing year. Too bad I knew nothing about peace or diplomacy. Why my grandmother wanted me to visit was a mystery to me; she could hardly expect me to love a man who had caused her so much pain. "Give him a chance," was all she'd said. "Let him tell you his side of the story himself." I'd lived with one side of the story my whole life—the true side. Living in a house filled with his absence, I had no desire to meet a man who was unconcerned with what his desertion had done to all of us. My mother and uncles had grown up without him. While he had been beginning anew in a warm and sunny climate, his abandoned family had struggled just to get by. I'd watched my mother and my uncles nurture a self-wounding hatred for him. Denying his existence wasn't easy. After all, he had left the three of them with his face. He was there in the reddish undertones of their skin, in the deep hollows of their cheeks, in the broad noses and the thin upper lips so unlike that of their mother. They could not discard him as easily as he could them. And, too, there was Titi Inez, his sister who still loved us as an aunt. She brought us stories of his doings. It was she who had told us when he moved from Bayamon to San Juan, when he bought a second car for his second wife. We couldn't shake stories of him. Even in his absence he was there, a mocking presence.

He'd been waiting outside the San Juan airport in a dusty green station wagon. As soon as he and Titi Inez saw each other they hugged and lapsed into Spanish, completely ignoring me, uncaring that I couldn't understand a word they said. I watched him while he ignored me, taking him in. The man I had pictured failed to merge with the flesh-and-blood one before me. His kinky hair, gnarled close to his head, was more gray than black, he was not as tall as my tallest uncle, and his face—plain, broad, and scowling—was red from overexposure to the sun. His ugliness was a disappointment. I'd assumed that a man capable of devastating one family, then picking up and jumping into another woman's arms without so much as a by-your-leave would be unbearably handsome, but my grandfather was not such a man. Perhaps he had been in 1952 when my poor, foolish grandmother had agreed to marry him, but he was no longer.

After I got in the car, he tossed our luggage into the backseat beside me and took off, driving faster than anyone I'd ever seen drive before, heedless of other drivers. Neither he nor Titi Inez wore seatbelts, but I strapped myself in. The entire car was hot. When I scooted across the seat the leather burned the backs of my legs, and when I reached for the seatbelt its fibers and metal clasp were hot to my touch. I fidgeted, wedging my hands beneath my thighs to block the heat.

He watched me in his rearview mirror. "What's wrong with her?" he asked my aunt in English. "Does she have to go?"

Answering for myself, I said, "I'm hot."

"You're on an island," he said, as if he were talking to an imbecile. "Puerto Rico is an island."

"So is Manhattan," I fired back. "It's not this hot there."

"So is Manhattan!" he repeated, laughing. He met my gaze in his rearview mirror, smiling approval at my cheeky comeback. "Yes, they did say you were smart. There, on the left. Roll down your window. You'll be cooler."

I rolled my window down, which only made the heat worse. The air came in a hot slap. My eyes felt suddenly dry. I rolled the window halfway back up and huddled away from it and the sultry air.

TITI INEZ LEFT the next day for Santurce, leaving me to a house full of relatives and strangers. My grandfather's children, Chalí and Cristina, took turns entertaining me. On the weekends they took me to Luquillo Beach, to Old San Juan, to El Morro, and to the movies to see *Big* and *Who Framed Roger Rabbit?* On weekdays they invited over Isi, a plump girl who knew no English but came with dolls and spoke the language of Barbie. Weekday evenings, they turned me over to my grandfather. Each evening I kept him company as he ate in front of the TV in the living room and watched baseball. After the game he played records, drilling song after song into me along with the names of musicians—Blades, Colon, Lavoe, Nieves, Palmieri, Puente—who meant nothing to me. He identified instruments: guiro, timbales, trumpet, bongos, cowbells, congas. I couldn't tell any of them apart. I was unused to hearing bands and orchestras. Occasionally my mother played *Earth, Wind & Fire* records, but most of the music I listened to at home was synthesized. Back at home, I had a Casio keyboard and at the press of a button I could have a host of instruments and prerecorded beats. I believed that you needed only an emcee, a deejay, two turntables, and speakers to make music. I had no experience with songs that required some ten or twenty people to make them a success.

These evenings, he offered no explanations for himself, unaware that I expected them. For him, I was something like Switzerland, a neutral entity, but one he hoped could be swayed. I went along with everything but laid in wait for him to reveal his true colors. I considered myself a spy in his house, a mole planted there to uncover his wickedness. Loyalty pushed my anger; love fueled my mistrust. At night, after everyone was asleep, I reconnoitered, walking barefoot through the one-level home, marveling at the ever-circling ceiling fan, the glass tables, the fat couches, the cool floor, the two cars parked by the side of the house, and the yard behind it overhung with coconut trees, wondering who my mother and uncles might have been if they'd lived in such a home raised amidst such privilege.

When the records failed to bring me over to his side, he drove us to Bayamon to see Héctor Lavoe sing live in concert.

Seeing the singer required our patience. We arrived only to wait in a disappointingly empty open-air arena. On all sides of me people spoke in Spanish. The audience thinned after the first hour, while we stayed and waited. As we waited, the people around us chanted the singer's name, demanding his presence. Dressed simply in a square-shouldered cotton shirt with vertical lace patterns down the front and tan slacks, my grandfather sat with his hands beating a pattern upon his knees, patient and excited. He cared nothing for the wait. Of all the musicians he made me listen to, this tardy man was his favorite. If we had to wait until morning for him to appear, we would.

I began to fidget. To keep me distracted, my grandfather had plied me with a piragua, but after I'd scooped the shaved ice into my mouth and sucked the cherry flavor out, I was bored once more. Finally, I asked, "Why is he so late?"

My grandfather placed a restraining hand on my knee and said, "He's worth it."

When I was about to argue the point, he cut me off, saying, "We have to forgive him, nena. He carries ghosts with him. Demons. He's a tormented man."

"Can't he get rid of them?" I asked.

"Nobody can escape them. You just have to stay out of their reach for as long as you can." My grandfather looked down at me then, catching sight of my fear. "Don't worry, nena," he said. "Just do like Héctor."

"What's that?"

"Give them one hell of a chase."

Sitting there in the open arena with the air close and hot, yet comforting, I asked what I wanted to know. Lowering my head, I focused on picking at the strings of my cutoff shorts and asked what happened between him and my grandmother.

"Your grandmother didn't work. She was lazy," he said. "My wife now works all of the time and she still had time to take care of the children."

It was an unfair comparison. His wife now was healthy, but my grandmother had been sick her whole life long. Two ectopic pregnancies in between the three children she'd delivered had ravaged her body, weakening her already ill frame. His wife now had the benefit of living near her family and could rely upon help with her children, whereas he'd dragged my grandmother away from Brooklyn and across multiple states where she knew no one, had no help, and had to do everything alone. In a time before daycare centers, my grandmother had been burdened and overwhelmed. His abandonment had impoverished us. Thirty years old with failing health and three children under the age of ten, my grandmother had been no match for the life to which he'd left her. Abandoned in an unfamiliar city with no support system and no income, she had been forced to wait until her mother and sisters could save up enough to send for her and her children. She'd returned to Brooklyn defeated and disheartened. By the time I knew her, she was old and weary. I wanted to point these things out to him, to let him know what he'd done to us, but instead, when I lifted my chin to answer, I asked, "Didn't you ever love her?"

"Shh," he said. "Héctor is coming to the stage."

THE SECOND CALL came five years later, after Héctor Lavoe's death brought my grandfather back to the United States, a place he'd abandoned in the '60s when he'd abandoned my grandmother and their three children, a place he'd vowed he would never return to. He came only for the funeral, stayed a mere three days, and was gone before we knew he'd even been in the country.

He called after he'd come and gone and was back in Puerto Rico, thinking us none the wiser. He filled me in on how illness and hard living had ruined the singer, ravaging his body, destroying his marriage, ruining his health. He told me Héctor Lavoe had wasted away in a hospital, that he had died hooked up to more machines than I could imagine. He talked for long minutes without ever once stopping, until—finally—he took a breath. He said, "What a terrible way for a man to die." He waited for me to soothe him as I had long ago that first time, but I would not say the words. It had taken effort just to stay silent on my end and listen without hanging up. My mother, uncles, and I were in the kitchen eating dinner when he called, and I didn't want them to know it was him. I had my own anger; I didn't need theirs. He had not called two years earlier when my grandmother died. If he had he would have known how the cost of her funeral had beggared us, sending my mother and uncles into a debt from which we had yet to resurface. When my mother informed him of the death, he had not cared. He had not sent so much as a sympathy card to show he was sorry that the mother of his first three children had died, but—over the phone now—there were tears in his voice for Héctor Lavoe, a man who was no relation to him at all, a man who had never even known my grandfather existed.

I refused to coddle his grief. I was in high school now, too old to play along. I suppressed a fresh stab of hurt and anger and pulled the long curling phone cord around the corner and into the living room. "How was the funeral?" I asked him. "Titi Inez told us you were there."

And I could see it too. I could see him there, a face among the crowd of mourners at Héctor Lavoe's funeral, crying and reaching out to touch the casket one last time. Easy to spot him among the throng of mourners who had taken their grief to the streets. Respectful in his mourning, dignified in his loss, my grandfather joined the funeral procession yet managed to walk apart. He would not have blended in with the howlers and the fainters. He would not have mourned like the others. There would have been no outpouring of emotions. He would not be among those screaming and crying, running for the hearse, reaching out to touch it, waving the bandera high or hoisting cardboard signs declaring love for Héctor, carrying pictures of him in his better days. See him walking silently, each step measured, content just to keep an inch of the car's black chrome within sight? Though it wouldn't have been noticeable to the casual observer, like the others, he too would have been crying. Unchecked, the tears would have formed two wet paths down his cheeks, but he would not have been embarrassed. He would not have tried to hide them or felt that they made him look weak. There would have been something remonstrative in his silent crying as, by example, he showed others the proper way to mourn. I could so easily see him there that way because it was the way I'd wanted to see him at my grandmother's funeral.

He said, "When the king dies, everyone goes out to the grave."

"He's just a man," I said.

"No, nena. Héctor was so much more than that for us."

"Why didn't you come to see us?" I asked. "You were close enough." The funeral had been in the Bronx; a train would have easily brought him to Brooklyn.

"Nena, you and I, we are all right, but I didn't think *they* would have wanted to see me." My grandfather kept quiet on his end, as if silence would bring me around to his way of thinking. I took exception to the way he referred to his children without saying their names but put himself on a first-name basis with the dead singer. Maybe they wouldn't have wanted to see him after he'd failed them at their mother's funeral, but if he had bothered to come, if he had made the smallest effort to try, maybe they would have allowed it anyway.

"You're right," I said, barely recognizing my own voice, hoarse with feeling. "They wouldn't have wanted to see you. And neither would I."

I hung up then, and I did not speak to my grandfather for many years.

HE RETURNED TO the States only once more, coming to New Haven for his youngest son Chali's wedding.

We were seated at different tables. My grandfather and his second family were seated up front. During the reception he made his way over to me. "Pretty soon it will be time for a wedding of your own," he predicted. He pulled out a chair that had been encased in a satin slipcover, the surplus fabric tied back in a loose yet tasteful bow. He seemed out of place sitting in such a chair. Though he wore a suit, he still looked like the man in the guayabera and the simple slacks.

"I'm in no rush," I told him, looking away from him to the glittering chandelier above our heads. I was twenty-five and, earlier that year, I'd bought a three-bedroom row home in Philadelphia, the city I'd moved to after college. I was giddy with my new status as a homeowner and burdened with repairs and renovations I had not foreseen. Despite the complications, I was enjoying the fact that I had bought the house by myself, needing no significant other's income to help me qualify. For the first time, I was not sharing space with roommates or relatives. I had no plans to ruin that with marriage. "Besides, I just bought my first house," I told him. "One adult step at a time."

I didn't tell him the real reason, that although I had not known him the first eleven years of my life, and though we had called a tenuous truce long ago, he had still managed to scar me. Seeing the damage one man could inflict had made me cautious. My grandfather's abandonment—his nonchalant justification for his behavior—had embedded itself into my skin, running deep as pores. Though I told myself I forgave him, his words were there behind every impossible test to which I subjected my prospective lovers, every hurdle over which I forced them to leap. The hurt he'd caused prompted my scrutiny of the men

I dated, made me look for that elusive thing, that invisible yet telltale sign, that signal that proclaimed the man akin to my grandfather. I would not be as foolish as my grandmother, believing simply in love and marriage, assuming that a man who fathered children would naturally love and want them.

When the couple seated to my left went to the open bar, my grandfather leaned across the table, his elbow dislodging a pat of butter from its dish. "Chalí says he's not going to play anything by *him*." My grandfather announced this as if it were a personal affront, something his son had done just out of spite.

The summer I'd stayed with them, Chalí had stayed mostly locked behind his bedroom door, practicing to be a deejay. I'd heard only the thrumming base of hip-hop blaring from his room as he played Run DMC and Big Daddy Kane. He'd never shown any interest in salsa. "Did you expect him to?"

"He could have just played one or two songs," he said. "He could have done it for me." My grandfather waved his weathered hand dismissively over the table's centerpiece. "Says he don't want nothing in Spanish. What are they playing now, nena? Do you know it?"

The deejay was playing a hit song from a popular all-girl group's second album. The song was meant for dance clubs and gym workouts. I was guilty of listening to it while on my elliptical machine. The lyrics castigated deadbeat men who indiscriminately accumulated bills and took advantage of their girlfriends. The song would have made an English teacher wince with the way it ignored the rules of grammar, but no one cared about that kind of thing nowadays. The song had been penned by the group's lead singer, a beauty whose father managed the group and who was rumored to soon be going solo. I pointed to all of the couples and singles who had risen from their tables and now crowded the dance floor. "They play this group on the radio all the time. Everybody likes them. They've won a Grammy."

"They must hand them out like *chicles* now. Look at all the beautiful songs Héctor had and how many albums it took him before he even got nominated. 1991," he said, refusing to concede. "Ay, nena, if Héctor

Lavoe could see me now. I have a son getting married, a granddaughter who owns her own house. Bought it herself, with nobody's help. Yes, I am man to be proud. Your house, it has many rooms?"

"It's no mansion," I said.

"I bet it's real nice."

I withdrew my wallet from my purse. "I have pictures."

"Other people put pictures of their kids in here," my grandfather chided, leaning closer to see the photos.

"One thing at a time," I said, ignoring the pointed criticism. I reminded myself that we had made our peace.

Years after I'd hung up on him, my grandfather had called to tell me about Tito Puente and El Conde's deaths six months apart. Then he'd sent me a cassette tape of all the songs we'd listened to together during the summer I'd visited. Listening to the tape of carefully selected songs, I'd remembered those nights as the closest we'd ever been. When he took the time to explain the music to me, I could not hate him. With the music between us, I could almost forget that he was the man who should have been in Brooklyn with us but had abandoned us and had a whole other family who got all of his time, care, and attention. Listening to the tape had reminded me that he was the only grandparent I had left, so I'd chosen to think of it as a peace offering, knowing an apology would never come from his mouth because if my grandfather had been the kind of man given to admitting his faults, no apology would have ever been needed.

"It's a fixer-upper," I said, showing him two pictures of the house.

My home was in West Philadelphia, in a neighborhood of row houses and Victorian twins and streets named after trees: Chestnut, Walnut, Locust, Pine, Spruce, and Cedar. I had a three-bedroom home in the middle of a block lined with trees and hedges. After college, I'd moved to Philadelphia because it seemed to me a more affordable version of New York, smaller but just as gray and loud and dirty and bustling.

Initially, I'd taken the before and after pictures in preparation of a new appraisal, but the pictures found their way into my wallet and remained. I liked knowing they were there.

The first picture was taken right after purchase, the second after I'd removed the carpet and made a few improvements. It was not a costly house; the mortgage was cheaper than my previous rent had been. There was no central air, no dishwasher, no modernity. The cabinets in the kitchen were old and darkened wood, too high above the counters. The kitchen windows had to be propped up in order to stay open. The walls were white-paneled wood. The basement was unfinished. The floors on the lower level were hardwood, and there were lighter streaks in the middle of the floor where the sun had bleached the wood. When I'd first moved in, the lower floor and stairs had been covered in green shag carpet that it had taken me four days to pull up. Knowing no better, I'd used the claw edge of a hammer to pry the carpet from the edges and bang down the nails and a box cutter for sections that became too unwieldy to roll. I hadn't thought about hiring someone to do the grunt work for me. I did the things I could do myself and made weekly trips to Home Depot. It hadn't occurred me to rely upon anyone other than myself.

"This is my favorite room," I said, showing him the "after" picture of my enclosed porch. "This is where I spend most of my time." I kept my books there, an armchair, umbrellas and phonebooks, and near-dying plants. I'd come into the house, pick up the mail, and sit in my armchair with my music and my work. In my living room, there was no television, only a stereo, a vintage record player, a pair of surround-sound speakers, and an entertainment center to hold all of the music. I would put on a rotation of CDs and listen to the music from where I sat in the enclosed porch, sitting there until the night became too dark or cold. It was like being in the house yet not in the house, and being outside yet not outside. Sitting in my armchair in the enclosed porch, I could hear the street outside, my neighbor's fourteen-year-old daughter bossing her friends and minding her little brother, cars passing. From where I sat in the enclosed porch, my house looked like an opportunity, as if everything was waiting to be done. I could see how much I'd already accomplished, how far I still had to go. It made me feel unlimited.

My grandfather took my wallet and held it in his hands, his elbow next to mine. In the distance, his second wife was signaling him to rejoin her and he was pointedly ignoring her beckoning hand. He flipped through the plastic sleeves slowly, carefully, looking at each one. He turned to me. "I can see you here," he said, examining me closely.

THE LAST CALL came tonight, while I was lying in bed beside a man I knew I would not marry.

The phone rang on the night stand closest to him.

"Hand it to me," I said when he seemed inclined to answer it. He lifted the cordless phone from its base and reached across our torsos to comply.

The phone's small screen revealed a 787 area code, a call from Puerto Rico, a call I assumed was from my grandfather to tell me another singer had died.

I clicked the talk button and Titi Cristina's voice came across clear and sad. "Your abuelo's gone," my grandfather's youngest daughter said. I listened as she told me of the heart failure that had taken his life. I promised her I would let my family know. Lying there, beside the man I knew I would never marry, I held myself still and tried to gather myself in, but before I knew it, I was crying.

"What's happened?" he asked.

"Someone very close to me died," I said, wiping my eyes. "I just found out."

He shifted under the covers and rose to a sitting position. "Who was it?"

"Someone very close to me," I repeated, failing to see how the specifics of idle curiosity preempted an offer of sympathy.

"I hope it wasn't your mom."

"No," I said, believing I'd supplied enough information.

He continued to stare at me as I cried. Finally he said, "I'm sorry to hear that."

"Thank you," I said. "I'd really appreciate it if you could leave."

After locking the door behind the man I knew I would never marry, I settled in my living room. I'd call my mother and my uncles in the morning and give them the news. I searched the drawers of my entertainment center for the handful of cassette tapes I still owned.

When I found them, I spread them out on the couch and searched until I found the one I wanted. I found the tape my grandfather had made me, pushed it into the tape deck and pressed play. I opened the door between my enclosed porch and my living room and sank into my armchair where I could hear both the music and the night.

ON MY LAST night in Puerto Rico, my grandfather called me into the living room. He said to me, "This is what you didn't hear."

He put on a record and positioned the two speakers on the floor so that they turned more fully toward us. "He would have sung this if they hadn't stopped him, but they didn't give him the chance." My grandfather's joy at attending the performance had been cut short when the concert ended abruptly. One minute, we could hear Héctor singing, and the next, the power on the stage had been shut off.

The song was slow to start. It began as if it were in a jungle or a forest, with the sounds of birds cawing, chirping, tittering, and screeching. Elephants trumpeted. In the distance, drums spoke and voices chanted, putting me in the mind of what I guessed African music sounded like. The song went on like this, growing without words. Then the horns kicked in, followed by a man's voice singing one lone word, stretching it to its limit, repeating it and pulling everything and more from the word he sang over and over. Without warning, drums rolled and all the instruments seemed to come in at once. I'd never heard any kind of song like it. Beneath the familiar instruments, I heard the sound of one I didn't know, a clanging like that of the small noisemakers sold on New Year's Eve. My grandfather identified it as the clave, the key, the rhythm, the heartbeat of all salsa.

The drums drove the beating of my heart. Seated on the floor in front of the couch, I felt that I was moving. My grandfather crouched beside the record player, eyes closed, beating the clave's rhythm against his leg. I feared the song would end, yet hoped it never would. I wanted the song to play, the drums to roll on and on. I picked up the album cover and stared at the man with the wide lapels and at the wide lenses of his tinted sunglasses. The day after we went to hear him, the singer jumped or fell from his hotel balcony's window. My grandfather kept silent vigil until he knew the singer would live, allowing no one to so much as even turn on the radio. Demons, my grandfather had said the singer had demons. When I listened to "Aguanile" that night, I knew what he meant. The chant of the song provided the means to chase the demons all away. I wondered if I had demons too, ghosts that needed expunging, and knew that we—both my grandfather and I—had our own ghosts that haunted us. It wasn't about me at all. He needed me to absolve himself. I was merely the youngest from that side of the family, the safest conduit. My mother and uncles, his first children, were too old and bitter to ever make their peace with him. What he didn't give to them, he'd tried to pass on to me. He was using me to get through to them and—that night—I allowed myself to be used.

"It's too bad they stopped him," my grandfather said. "I wish you could have heard this song on the stage." That night, in spite of everything, I wished it too.

Now We Will Be Happy

TOSTONES MAKE NO excuses. Platanos—plantains—burn in hot oil, their golden edges blackening before she remembers them. Smoke invades her nose and throat, a dark burning smell of food and melting metal, the smell of the frying pan's handle overheating. She is careful to keep her distance when she turns the fire off. She gives the oil time to resettle, steering clear of its pop and hiss, knowing too well just how long burns take to heal.

This is the price of looking. She'd ignored the frying tostones for her own beckoning face, following her reflection as it wavered in the chrome hood above the stove. Despite the dullness of the metal, the bruises showed through clearly. She'd thought they wouldn't show this time, yet an hour after Pedro left, the faint marks darkened, unfurling like blooms across her face.

Rosa plucks the tostones from the pan with her spatula and slides them one by one onto the wooden tostoñera, where the oil seeps into the fibrous threads, drenching the wood dark wet. Centering the golden wedge, she lowers the handle, forcing the two wooden ends to meet, crushing the plantain flat. The tostones that emerge are hopeless. Instead of perfect golden discs, they are charred beyond recognition, black around the edges and raw at the center. Pedro would never eat them, but Yauba is not so demanding.

She can't let him see her like this.

THEY HAD ONLY to swallow, only to taste.

Across the serving line—on the other side of the sneeze guard, the residents came and went without ever once raising their eyes. Taking no notice of Yauba, these international girls—Japanese, Italian, and German mostly—who had come here for school, lifted fingers and pointed to what they wanted, held their plates up to the gloved hands that dished their helpings. Their lodgings, their meals were all covered. Their rooms had been supplied furnished and were cleaned weekly by housekeeping. They did not have to clean. They did not have to cook. They had only to be on time for meals served three times daily. They had only to take a tray, gather silverware, and decide between meat or vegetarian options, only to walk down the line and select their dessert from ramekins of pudding, gelatin, or cubed fruit. If ever they looked past the clear-gloved hand and the long slotted spoon, it was only to ask about sodium levels and ingredients to which they were allergic. What did they know of corrugated metal and zinc roofs, these girls who had never to see, never to speak, only to swallow, only to taste?

Rosa is nothing at all like them, Yauba reminds himself as he scans the room of women oblivious to his presence, and finds himself free for the day from feeding the privileged. Fresh from the manager's office, Yauba passes back through the residence's cafeteria, through a room full of women who pay him no notice, who see him not at all. Rarely does he see the view from this side of the serving line. To his way of thinking, the place where the women eat is far more "dining hall" than "cafeteria." There are no long wooden tables or stackable chairs. Each chair is covered in fabric, each table seats only four. Linen tablecloths are topped with squares of glass, weighted down by vases full of fresh flowers. Women walk across patterned carpet and make their way down the serving line. An elderly woman sitting at the end of the line, behind the one cash register, checks the residents' names off her list when they show their trays. In this expansive space, the women sit, eat, linger, and laugh over the food Yauba prepares.

But he has not prepared today's food. Today he has been suspended. Before he could even change into his checks and clock in, Jim called him into his office and gave him the news that he could not stay and work. Connie, the new hire in the kitchens, had accused several of the men of sexual harassment, and Jim was putting them on ice until he got to the bottom of it. She had not named Yauba specifically, had not actually accused any of the men by name. The kitchen workers were a brown coalition of Caribbean men from Puerto Rico, the Dominican Republic, Cuba, Venezuela, and Colombia and she knew none of them by name.

Yauba pushes aside his anger at Connie, who knew nothing about cooking—wanting the hotel pans where the half pans belonged and using vegetable cutting boards for meat—who turned her mouth down at the corners whenever the men spoke Spanish, vain enough to believe that a practice they'd adopted years before her arrival was now done with the intention of making her feel uncomfortable. He pushes aside anger at Jim's underhandedness and Connie's cowardly act of accusing him without positive identification, at the inconvenience of having to ride all the way back to Brooklyn when Jim could have saved him the trip with a phone call. He pushes aside his anger at Jim for finally making him Second Cook, but never raising his salary, for holding the bait of a pay raise over his head while making him do the inventory, the meal planning, and the budgets—the work of the food director and head cook—all on his regular salary. Two years ago Jim had promised to make him assistant manager when the position opened up and then passed him over for a twenty-five-year-old towheaded boy. Thanks to the Jones Act, no Puerto Rican is an immigrant, a fact Jim always pretends not to know. He hates to pay him his due, give him his rights, treat him like the citizen he is. Anger does him no good in a place like this, not when Jim can take his salary and use it to hire three immigrants and pay them under the table.

Thoughts of the restaurant he dreams of owning push aside the anger. One day he will go home. Once there, he will open a restaurant. He will call it "Celina's" and everyone will come and eat. One day these things he puts up with will be worth it. He can see it now. It will be nothing like this dining hall. It will be simple and suited to its climate. There, the whitewashed walls. There, the big square-cut windows. And overhead—just there—the ceiling fan with its wings slowly circling. With each revolution of the imaginary fan his anger ebbs, until it is safe for him to go and see Rosa. He has made a promise never to visit her angry.

YAUBA LIFTS A toston, withered and black, to his mouth and tests it between strong white teeth, a jeweler testing gold. "Not bad for your first try," he says. "But maybe we should start again."

Rosa hands him a fresh green plantain and sets the flame under a new, clean pan. With a thick-handled knife, Yauba pries the tough skin away from the starchy meat inside. Then he cuts the plantain into wedges and drops them on their sides into the sizzling oil. With a steady hand, he rolls them, coating them evenly. She watches, transfixed by the quiet grace of his hands, the strength and steadiness of his fingers. In a shirt unbuttoned at the wrists, its cuffs turned back from the dark skin, Yauba seems too rugged to be cooking, too quietly assured to be standing in the kitchen beside her. She did not plan to desire this man with eyes as dark as coffee beans, set in a face weathered by time and age. His face has none of the masculine prettiness she has been taught to call beauty. He is not handsome like Pedro, not guapo. He does not have Pedro's height or bulk. Yauba is skinny, flaco, thinner than thin. No, she did not plan to desire Yauba, but now all she wants is to live beneath the touch of his hands.

"You cooked yours too long. Each one should be like a little bit of sunshine," Yauba says, after crushing a plantain slice between the tostoñera and sliding it back into the oil. Six yellow circles sizzle in the frying pan, simmering beneath a layer of oil, hardening and crispening. When Yauba removes them from the pan, each toston has a golden face; the thready veins that run along the side of the plantain, now flat, look like emanating rays of sun. Each toston looks as if it is smiling.

When they come together, they do not talk about their day. He does not tell her Jim sent him home early on an unwarranted suspension; she does not say how many layers of makeup it takes to conceal. They forget the hours that have come before and the people that have come between them. This time, when the tostones come out, they are perfect. Yauba places them on a paper towel before her and Rosa pats them dry. He sprinkles salt from his palm onto the chips and the two lift the still-hot tostones to their mouths, not bothering with plates, eating them together as they lean over the sink, eating them hot, salty, and crisp.

"Who made you like kitchens?" she asks.

"I don't *like* kitchens," he says, thinking she has made it sound as if he is not a man.

"I didn't mean it that way."

"I've been cooking since an early age," he says. "Almost forever."

"Who taught you to make Spanish food? Your mother?"

"It's not Spanish food," he says, an edge in his voice. "The only thing Spanish about Puerto Rican food is the onions, the olives, and the garlic. These plantains came over from Africa on the same boats as the slaves."

"What slaves?" she asks, wondering how Yauba and everyone else knew so much more than she.

"The slaves that brought the plantains, yams, okra, and gandules. The Tainos had yuca, corn, lerén, yautia, guava, soursop. Our food is *criolla*, just like the people, a mix of all three cultures. Just like us." She hears in his voice what she sees in the eyes of men whenever they spot the bandera waving from a car's antenna, a caressing love for a place she has never seen and cannot call to mind.

"So who taught you?" she asks again. "Your mother?"

"Not my mother," he says, thinking of the aunt who took care of him and of her last days when he returned the favor. With age, his Titi Celina's hands had become arthritic and her taste buds eccentric. She would call in the morning for flan; at night she'd ask for eggs. She dreamed the dreams of a gourmand, awaking to ask for hams and roasted pork shoulders, pastelillos and pumpkin flan, rice and pigeon peas, apples cored and stuffed with raisins, dishes her hands could no longer prepare. "Someone else."

Rosa waits in silence to see if he will say more. She does not care that she is being unreasonable, that he had a life before he met her, that she is the one with a spouse—she is jealous now of the mystery woman from his past who'd taught him to stand here beside her in a kitchen and feel completely at home. "She did a good job," she says.

"Come see me tomorrow," he says. "I'll make lunch."

These are not the rules, and well he knows it. They are to meet only here, only on the fourth floor, only in her apartment, where he can pretend to be visiting others he knows, where no one will notice or care when he enters or exits the building.

"I'm going to see my parents tomorrow."

"Come after."

These are not the rules, and though she knows she shouldn't do what he asks, she knows for certain that she will.

KIDNEYS CONSUME THE lives of Rosa's parents and Rosa doesn't remember it any other way. Weak kidneys keep her father in bed and her mother distracted. By the time she was in fourth grade, her father had become a prisoner to the back bedroom and her mother had become his caretaker. The señora left the house only for groceries, prescriptions, and trips to the doctor. Made wary by too many misdiagnoses, her mother accompanied her father to his thrice-weekly treatments. First, the doctors said he was anemic, then that he had gallstones. It took two years of her father vomiting up what looked like coffee grounds, two years of him sleeping more and more hours a day and still waking tired, two years of pain every time the ball of a joint pressed into a socket before they discovered one of his kidneys was only 5% functional. Though she little understands anything about the illness, her parents can speak at length about urea, phosphate binders, and degenerative bone disease.

"Mom? Did you know there were slaves in Puerto Rico a long time ago?"

"Hmm?" The señora listens to her daughter with one ear as she works to cook a meal that will not cause her husband anguish. The señora is careful, so careful to limit the potassium, phosphorous, and sodium levels of the food she prepares, so careful that Rosa feels like a nuisance come to bother her. Only months since she and Pedro moved out, yet each time Rosa visits, her mother looks more peaked and tired.

"Mom. Slaves. Puerto Rico. Did you know?"

Her mother runs water over a pot filled with potatoes, then sets the pot on the stove's backburner, hoping to reduce their potassium levels by soaking. She looks up from the potatoes, brushes hair out of her face. "Of course," she says, eyeing her daughter strangely. "Everybody knows that."

"How?"

Her mother takes Rosa's arm, unfolds it at the elbow, and holds her own arm close beside her daughter's. She gestures to their brown skin. "Did you think Spaniards and Indians could make this by themselves?"

Rosa adjusts her sleeve, tugging it over the dark marks. She offers to help with the meal, but her mother doesn't need her.

"I've got it under control," the señora says. "Can I get you anything?"

"I'm fine," Rosa says, wondering why visits have to go like this, why she has to be addressed formally, why there is never anything she can do to help, why she has to be served like a guest in a restaurant, rather than treated like a daughter come home. "Do you need me to run to the store and get anything for you?"

The señora shakes her head. She fixes a plate of cauliflower and boiled chicken legs.

"Is Dad up? I think I'll go say hi."

"Now is not a good time for hi. I'm getting ready to bring him his lunch. I have a hard enough time trying to make him eat. If he sees you, he'll get too excited and I'll never be able to get anything in him." The señora pours half a glass of 7-Up and takes the glass and plate in hand. "I'll be right back."

Minutes pile upon one another before Rosa makes her way down the hall to her old bedroom, tired of waiting for her mother's return.

In the months that she and Pedro have been gone, her old bedroom has been turned into a laundry room of sorts. Stacks of folded, clean linens sit on her old bed and wet clothing hangs over the headboard. In the space between the bed and an armoire Pedro insisted they leave behind, her mother has erected an ironing board. Rosa lifts the tall can of starch and fingers the long-sleeved shirt hanging by its collar off the ironing board's narrow end. This is her father's shirt, and even though he has nowhere to go, nowhere to be, her mother still presses and starches his shirts. The sleeve is cool to the touch. Rosa runs her fingers down the empty sleeve, holding the cuff and swinging it. She has thought of leaving Pedro and coming back home, but her parents have enough worries. If she came home, she'd have to tell her father why, and that she cannot do.

How long since she has known the safety of the four walls of this room? Rosa sits gingerly on the edge of her old bed far from the abandoned doll lying on the pillow and remembers that she has not known safety in this room.

HE DOESN'T HAVE to look down at his hands; he knows what he is doing. He is as at home with the polished steel and aluminum equipment, with the bain-marie, the hotel pans, the six pans, and the rivets as he is with the caldera, pilón, and tostoñera. He dissolves a cake of raw brown sugar into a pitcher of water to make agua de panela. He fluffs the rice, he chills the flan.

Whether here or on the job, there is always something to be prepped, stirred, steamed, basted. That is why he has devoted so little time to his décor. Now that Rosa is coming over, Yauba sees everything with new eyes, her eyes. It is not an apartment a woman would like. There are no plush sofas or overly large leather chairs. No graceful touches. The only flourishes—if they can be called such—are in his kitchen where he keeps his implements. Silver knives gleam, hung with precision. His apartment is as neat and lifeless as a barracks. How bare, how small she makes his apartment seem, how tiny his life before her.

He should have pictures for his walls; he should have plants. Something—anything—to make her feel welcome, to make her want to stay. There is not enough time for him to run out and buy anything. He will have to make do. He has been taught to make use of any and everything. His titi found a use for every part of a pig, making mondongo out of tripe and morcilla out of pig's blood. She'd taught him to give thanks, make do, and take nothing for granted. His titi could take a seed and turn it into a snack. He could and would take nothing for granted, least of all the love of a married woman he cannot stop himself from seeing.

Inside the refrigerator's vegetable bin, he finds fresh cilantro and parsley. He fills two plastic cups with water and floats the herbs on top. He places the cups on his windowsills. There, that should do it. Now he has plants.

AFTER THE FIRST mouthful of arroz con gandules, Rosa knows that this is love. At first she thinks the love overwhelming her—triggered by the taste of the rice, pigeon peas, and green olives—is for the dish and not the man, but after chewing and swallowing, she knows better. It is the man whose hand holds the spoon that she loves. It is a shame he is not her husband.

"What do you think?" Yauba asks.

At first she doesn't wish to speak, thinking that words will make the all-consuming love go away. Tentatively, she says "Delicious," and—wonder of wonders—the love is still there.

It is not the food he has prepared, nor the way he holds out the spoon for her to taste—as if she is a critic with a discerning palate—that makes the moment special. It is the words that precede the spoon, the sentences that come before the swallow. Yauba brings the spoon to her lips and says, "My aunt—my titi Celina—taught me how to cook. This was her favorite. When I open my restaurant, I'm naming it after her. This dish will be my specialty."

As they eat, he tells her about living with his aunt. Rosa can see the small boy that was Yauba sweeping dust from the walkway in front of his aunt's house. Yauba makes her see the rainy nights, hear the patter of the rain on the corrugated metal, the ping of water droplets against the zinc rooftop. How cool the air that comes afterward, lingering at the windows, refreshing him after a long day of errands and chores. She sees the concrete walls, his aunt's Santería shrine at the back of the house, with its gifts of corn and coffee for the orichás.

She envies Yauba his stories, covets his memories.

Her own memory is of nighttime chatter. When they thought her asleep, her parents would converse in soft-spoken Spanish. With their door left open and the volume of the television turned down low, they would talk late into the night. Betrayed by the refuge her parents sought in the intimacy of their private language, she'd crack her door open at night after her mother had shut it and fall asleep to the incomprehensibility of words, believing that if she listened hard enough, eventually she would understand all that was being said.

The girl she had been had longed to know what her parents knew, but the woman she became had long since given up. Her parents weren't telling, and her husband, Pedro, used her ignorance against her.

Yauba believes he has distanced her with his ramblings. "I'm boring you. I didn't mean to go on. How about some music?"

Though she would rather hear more, she joins him at the stereo. He fiddles with the radio tuner, switching among three all-Spanish stations. "Ah, this is a good one. 'Ahora Seremos Felices.'" He turns to her, smiling. "Know what that means?"

She says no with a smile, feeling no embarrassment, smiling simply because he is smiling too.

"It means 'now we will be happy,'" he tells her. "It's Rafael Hernández."

Even she knows of El Jibarito. He lived among a stack of record albums crowded into a milk crate in the bottom of her parents' closet. He lived among a host of musicians—Lavoe, Nieves, Palmieri, Puente—her parents listened to only in her absence, only when they thought her asleep.

"It's beautiful."

"Dance with me," Yauba says, but she doesn't know the steps. She gives him her hand and lets him show her. Yauba pulls her into arms stronger than they seem, and the two are not really dancing, are barely even moving. She is merely swaying in the circle of his arms, following as he directs her movements. He holds her steady with subtle pressure but without force, the same way he steadies the knife for the tostones. Her feet barely lift from the ground; there is just a subtle shifting of weight as she drifts between the safety of his arms and the words.

As they dance, Yauba sings words which have no meaning for her. Her parents should have told her the things Yauba already knew. Instead, they'd kept their secrets. Everyone knew more than her, it seemed. Whenever she asked Pedro, he used the language against her, wielding it like a weapon, mocking and ridiculing her, telling her to "look it up," as if she were a lazy child attempting to cheat her way out of vocabulary homework. He never missed an opportunity to let her know he'd gotten less than he bargained for in marriage to her.

But how can she ever look it up when she doesn't know where to start? She is tired of not knowing, tired of being left out.

"Cariña, why are you crying?"

When he reaches out to touch her cheek, she flinches. She can't help it. "I want to go," she says.

Immediately, he releases her. "I would never hurt you."

"I just wish I could see it," she says. "I want to go with you when you open your restaurant."

More than anything, it is what he wants too. "I'll take you," he says. "I promise."

"I wish we could go now," she says. Come what may, she decides that she will have this one thing. She will take Yauba's love and keep it all to herself.

"We can."

When she raises dubious eyes to him, he says only, "Wait here."

TEN MINUTES LATER, he returns for her and leads her down the hallway. She thinks he intends to take her to his bedroom, but he bypasses it and brings her into the bathroom. "What are you doing?" she asks.

"We're going to Luquillo Beach," he says. He hands her a tee shirt and a pair of shorts similar to the ones he has changed into. "You can put these on."

She steps out of her sandals and lifts her dress over her head. When she has changed clothing, she allows him to guide her into the half-filled tub. He dips a hand into the water and snaps his fingers beneath the surface, creating a wrinkle of water. The ripple becomes the ruffling of wind over water, the kisses of waves.

With her eyes closed, she can see what Yauba describes. The warm tub water is the Atlantic Ocean, lapping at the edge of the beach. The bare bathroom lightbulb is the warm sun in the sky beating down upon her. Yauba joins her in the water, making it rise to the rim of the tub as he settles in behind her.

"One of us should stop us," she says, though she knows it is now too late.

"Not me," Yauba says.

"Not me," says Rosa.

Her back to his chest, they lie back in the water, bathing in Yauba's makeshift ocean. Saying nothing, he washes each of her fingers and each web of skin in between. He lifts her arms and washes the dark marks tenderly. He touches her without lewdness, makes her forget all about Pedro, makes her know that bruises can heal. The bruises fall from her the way rain, gathered in the large folds of banana leaves, pours off in a rush when it has become too heavy to hold.

When he is done and she is cleaner than she has ever been, he tells her the meanings of all the words she has ever wanted to know.

Bodega

ONE HOUR BEFORE they open their bodega to the morning crowd, Nelida rolls up the store's accordion gates. Each day, when her husband sweeps the night's trash from the front of their store, she comes and stands and stares at the early morning sky. This early in the morning the sky poses little threat, yet she watches it anyway. With padlocks in hand she faces the day, looking out over the brown bricks of the four-story housing projects across the street while her husband sweeps the concrete step, unmindful of her, used to her staring by now.

They are the only two out this early. The other proprietors—Italian, Arab, Jewish, and Chinese merchants—are nowhere to be seen. Soon enough, they will drive in from their homes in Staten Island, Manhattan, and the nicer parts of Brooklyn. By the time they arrive and open, Nelida will have made the coffee, buttered the rolls, and sold the cigarettes that draw the morning crowd. She will have ushered out the schoolchildren who linger in the aisles fondling the snack cakes, and she will have sent her grandson off to school. By the time the other stores on the block open, the sun will be out and the sky will look like a sky, not the way it looks to Nelida now, like an ocean flung high above her head.

Steadily vigilant, she sweeps her glance up and down the street. On either side of the projects directly facing their store, identical housing complexes stretch out to the corners of Bradford and Van Siclen Avenues. The three blocks of projects—four buildings to each block—house the majority of their customers. On her side of Pitkin Avenue lies the neighborhood's commerce. Three blocks of nothing but storefronts. To her right the dry cleaner's, liquor store, candy store, and botánica will soon open for the day. To her left the barber shop, Chinese restaurant, and discount store will remain closed a few hours more. On the corner—between it all—their own bodega stands aloof, easily distinguished by the yellow awning embossed with red letters, which boasts of its presence: ICE CREAM, CANDY, SODAS, ICE COLD, COLD CUTS, CIGARETTES, BEER, WE ACCEPT WIC HERE.

Unlike the Arab brothers who run the store on Van Siclen or the Dominican owners of the bodega on Bradford, Nelida and her husband do not sell hot food or run numbers. They do not own slot machines or scoop Italian ices. They refuse to stay open all hours of the night. They sell just enough, careful not to overextend themselves just to compete. They prefer to go to bed at a decent hour. They like to spend the evenings with their grandson, to sit with him and discover who he is, find out what he likes. He has just recently discovered WWF wrestling. Now he begs to stay up late in order to watch Ricky "The Dragon" Steamboat, Macho Man Randy Savage and George "The Animal" Steel. To keep the boy company, Nelida has watched several of these wrestling matches with her grandson, marveling at the theatrics, incredulous when a tubby bald man with a green tongue and dog collar leaves the match to run around the wrestling ring chasing a woman he calls Elizabeth. It is a little too King Kong for her and so obviously fake; yet her grandson Esteban watches with the absorption only a child could have, greedily and believing easily.

So easily could her little family have ended up on the other side of the street. Sheer diligence kept them from floundering when they'd first arrived in New York. With his careful and cautious ways, her husband had anticipated difficulties and prepared accordingly, working to ensure that nothing caught them unawares. He'd accounted for everything but the sky, which came and beckoned their son with its promises, luring him away and back to Puerto Rico. Now Nelida begins her day only after she has seen the sky for herself. She takes no one's word for it. Dutifully, she keeps close watch on the treacherous sky. She never turns her back on it.

Once his sweeping is finished, her husband hands her the broom. Before he can head down to the storeroom, she stops him. "Something tells me you have a letter," Nelida says. "A little bird, maybe."

"Neli, it's too early for this."

"You would tell me, no?"

"Of course," he says, but his eyes won't meet hers. They slide away, lighting on the curb. He pretends he sees trash and takes the broom from her once more, vigorously sweeping the sidewalk. "Why don't you go inside? It's too cold for you out here."

"Yes," she says, unwilling to argue. "Too early." So early in the day and she has already forced her husband into such an unnecessary lie. He doesn't have to confirm that a letter has come to them. She already knows. The truth was in the wordless way he'd come to bed last night, the listless way he held her as they'd drifted off to sleep.

She rubs her arms where the cool air has made them pimply. She has always found the mainland too cold, too wet, too windy, especially now in the spring. Now that she has seen the sky for herself, there is nothing to keep her, and it is indeed too early to push him. She pushes open the bodega's door and the jingle of small bells announces her presence in the empty store. It is too early in the day for disagreements, too early for protective lies. It is too early for children to be out and about and too early for workers and other respectable adults to be milling in the streets. It is too early for anything but the opening of a store and the effort such openings take.

INSIDE, THE STORE is warm. A faint and stale breeze wafts from a dusty industrial-sized fan standing in the corner next to the brown plastic cartons containing loaves of Wonder and Home Pride bread. Refrigerator-sized coolers full of beer, juice, Maltas, milk, and sodas line the wall opposite the counter and aisles of dusty cans and boxes and jars fill the space in between. They keep the store stocked with items that the folks from back home would want—Goya products, tins of guava paste, chicharrones, octopus sold in oil or in garlic sauce, sofrito, recaito and achiote, packets of sazon sin pimienta or con saffron—items not always carried by the local supermarket. At the end of the aisle hang bags of pork rinds and dried plantain chips.

The hour before the store opens is the quietest hour of her day. Once they open their doors to the public, there will be no peace, there will be no quiet. The morning traffic will be filled with civil servants heading off to their jobs working for the post office, the transit authority, and department of motor vehicles. The afternoon will be filled with children pushing and shoving. The hours in between will be filled with the wanderers who come in with no intention to buy. Each day, in the quiet hour before the bodega opens, before the store becomes filled with young girls with tattoos on their arms and babies on their hips, before the endless round of unemployed men who buy their cigarettes one at a time, before the afterschool influx of children buying chips and snack cakes one quarter at a time, before she begins a day of making change, selling loosies, and cashing WIC checks, Nelida leaves her body behind in the bodega and lets her soul fly out across the Atlantic Ocean, sailing home to Puerto Rico. But today there is no time to make the trip when there is a letter to be found. Somewhere inside the store her husband has hidden the latest letter from the son they have not seen in far too long. Six years ago, they'd struck a bargain with their son, agreeing to raise Esteban for him while he served in the army. Instead of returning after completing his service commitment, he reneged and relocated to Puerto Rico, the place they'd left when he was fourteen years old. Now he taunts them with news of his new life in Humacao and pretends he is never coming back.

Nelida makes her way down the aisle, displacing non-perishables, seeking the letter behind cans of red beans, pigeon peas, and menudo. She watches herself in the small mirror placed at the end of the aisle to discourage theft. The woman she sees searching for a letter among the rows of canned goods is a distortion of the woman she knows herself to be. This Nelida is older, fatter, grayer. This Nelida's roots show at her scalp and temples, where the auburn rinse is fading. When she was young and vital, she had believed that her body would always be firm and that each day would be as sunny as the one which preceded it. She'd believed that love and opportunity would always be abundant and she'd believed herself to be more knowledgeable than the women who'd raised her. She hadn't believed her mothers or titis wise, hadn't believed they could tell her anything about life. Now she knows better. Her husband had never intended to stay in Puerto Rico. He had never cared about the sky and the sun. He was unimpressed by the way the leaves of the coconut trees waved toward the sun, as if someone were stretching a paintbrush up to the sky. When the two were newly married, he had teased her by saying that she looked like a tourist, staring at the sky every day like it was the first time she had ever seen it. When they'd met, he'd been working down by the beaches and malls, selling piraguas—flavored ices—during the day and driving taxis at night. Even then, he'd been planning. It was just her luck to have fallen in love with a restless man. She'd loved a man who was a hurricane in his youth, always swirling and moving, uprooting things and carrying them along with him. She is too old now for hurricanes, too weary to twist her body into a semblance of willingness, too disillusioned to make meaningless sounds of pleasure. Now, between the two of them they share a comfortable peace instead of a whirl of passion. Now they have the quiet hours that come after they have closed up the store and Esteban is spread out in front of the television despite their countless attempts to get him to go to bed. Nelida would trade in all of the nights of passion that she and her husband had spent fruitlessly trying for a brood of children if only she could have one quiet hour in the living room with her husband, her son, and her grandson—all of her small family—sitting together comfortably. For her, it would be enough. If her son would return home to them, she could have her one wish. Each letter he sends could be the one that tells her what she wants to hear.

IT IS A store for a letter to get lost in, so crammed and full.

Naturally, the letter will be well-hidden. She knows better than to look in the obvious places. Certainly it will not be upstairs where there are too few places to stash it. While making coffee for the morning rush, Nelida searches for the letter beneath a stack of invoices behind the counter, rifling through the papers and finding nothing. She will know the letter upon sight. Its envelope will have been treated carefully, its seam gently opened, its flap tucked back into its body, unlike the envelopes containing invoices. Though her husband has already read it, she can expect nothing but silence from him, knowing he won't say a word until he thinks the time is right. He calls this secrecy his way of protecting her, believing he is doing her a favor by intercepting the mail. He blames the letters for her bad heart, claims that they worsen her condition. He had justified hiding the last letter by arguing it was for her own good, saying, "His letters only cause you pain."

"You don't need to tell me about pain," she'd answered.

"These letters are not good for your heart. I don't want you to get overexcited."

It was true, the doctors did warn against too much excitement, but Nelida didn't lend their opinions any weight. They blamed the foods she ate and didn't listen when she tried to tell them the real cause of her heartache. How could they know that each time she'd lost a child, she'd lost a little piece of her heart? The doctors didn't believe in broken hearts, but Nelida knew that there truly was an imperceptible tear in the muscle that was her heart. She'd felt the tiny ripping pains, the fibrous threads flung loose. If the doctors couldn't understand something as simple as that, she had no use for them.

Such a big fuss over such a small thing, a letter. She'd told her husband the same thing she told the doctors, that she could handle it. She would rather have this sliver of communication than nothing at all. She had learned to look past the words on the page, to ignore the insolence and disregard the disrespect. She had become adept at reading between the lines, bypassing the insults, and remembering instead the child she'd had to chase out of her kitchens, the little boy who'd begged for the pegao at the bottom of the pot of rice. Any mother could see through the taunts and jibes to the vulnerable boy lashing out. Soon he would tire of the taunts and long to see the son he had left behind. One day soon he would realize that they could all manage much easier if he were there to help. Soon he would return to his son and his parents and ease all of their burdens. In the meantime, Nelida cultivated patience and clung to her convictions. Even though the room was now used by her grandson, she took care to keep it just the way her son had left it. She made sure to tell Esteban good stories about his father so that once her son returned the two could pick up right where they'd left off.

If he would only return, he'd see how hard she'd worked to keep everything intact.

She looks for the letter under the cash register's tray and finds only the colorless paper money of food stamps.

Her husband said it was ingratitude that kept their son away, that their careless handling of love and their overindulgence was what made him treat them so shabbily, so assured was he of their inexhaustible forgiveness. But when there was only one son and a mother knew there would be no others, what else was there to do but coddle? It wasn't indulgence that kept him away. No, Nelida knew the truth. It was fear, fear that the bodega would consume his life, fear that he would become as old and trapped as his parents by four leased walls and the hope of prosperity. So easily could the store become one's prison. So easily could one be jailed inside by the boxes upon boxes, cartons upon cartons, and crates upon crates of inventory and merchandise. She and her husband could spend hours at a time in the store dusting, loading the coolers with sodas, bottles of beer, cartons and gallons of milk and still have more to do. She hadn't wanted her son to become a prisoner to the store the way they were. There was no one to whom they could hand the reins when they needed a break. There was no one to run the store but them. They were owned by the bodega, unable to take a few days off because they couldn't afford to lose customers. It fed her ego to pretend their customers would be lost if she and her husband ever took a vacation, that their customers would flounder and miss the couple who gave many of them credit and let them use food stamps to buy non-food items like toilet paper and cat food, but she was pragmatic enough to be sure that as soon as they closed the store and took a vacation, their customers would walk the extra two blocks down to the next bodega or go all the way to the C-town supermarket, taking their money with them and—like her son—they would never come back.

She has looked everywhere and the letter is nowhere to be found. Surely, then, her husband has hidden it on his person, keeping it close, tucking it somewhere between shirt and skin.

Here in this pre-opening hour, there is no one to ask her for change, no requests for credit and tabs to tide folks over until the first or the fifteenth of the month, there is no need to monitor the corners of the aisles where the addicts like to linger—and no letter to be found. Here in this pre-opening hour lies the peace of mind it takes to see the rest of the day through, and she has relinquished it for a letter that has eluded her search. When this hour is over she will not have a minute to herself to think. There will be no quiet for her in which to hear her own thoughts. This is the hour, this is the time when she has the world all to herself, the only time when she has herself to herself. Upstairs in their apartment, she belongs to her husband and grandson, her small but precious family. She paints the walls in the rooms of their home with her love. She funnels it into her grandson with his morning cereal, splashes it on with his milk, packs it in with his lunch. Down here in the bodega, she belongs to her neighborhood. Six blocks worth of people come to this store. Six blocks teeming with civil servants, drug addicts, proprietors, clerks, home attendants, truants, and old folks eking a living off meager ssi and disability checks come in daily. Every morning the man who owns the barbershop four doors down wants a buttered roll and his coffee black with two sugars. The man who runs the video rental store comes in every few hours for a tropical fruit soda. Six blocks worth of regulars, six blocks worth of needs. They call her by a multitude of names. She is sometimes, but rarely, Mrs. Torres, Ma'am, or Miss. More often than not she is Excuse Me, Can You Extend Me Some Credit Until the Next Time?, How Much is This?, and How Come You All Don't Carry . . . ? Down here, there is a wall of Plexiglas that rises up from the counter, a clear, solid, thick bulletproof barrier that protects her from the unpredictable and sudden violence of the disenfranchised yet is useless in shielding her from the anger and the resignation, the hunger and the need that follows each patron in, ringing louder than the bells that jingle overhead. They hand those feelings over to her along with their WIC checks, their food stamps, their cash, their coin, and what they take from her when she hands over their bags and slides their change across the counter only they can know.

When this hour is over, she will turn on her vigilance, keeping one eye on the customers in front of her and the other eye on the security mirrors. She will scrutinize the face of each young male attempting to buy cigarettes or beer, looking for telltale signs of boyhood.

This would all be so much easier if only they had some help. If only their son would come back to them and shoulder some of the burden's weight. Then she could have more minutes, more hours even to herself and she would not need to crave this ounce of solitude as fiercely as she does. She would not need to cram her desire into this one quiet hour of which she has needlessly wasted three quarters.

There is still time left. Time enough for her.

Fifteen minutes remain of the precious hour, but perhaps there is time enough for her to make her trip and salvage something good from these mere minutes.

As the sky glows faintly with the rising sun, Nelida lets her soul fly to her island across the ocean and take her where it will.

SHE FINDS HERSELF in Rio Piedras, the neighborhood of her childhood, standing on the street where she'd once lived, in front of a house which she cannot recall. A small handwritten sign stands in the window, propped in front of lacy white curtains:

Se Vende Limber
—tamarindo
—coco
—guayaba
—leche
—frambuesa

—limón

—maní

—crema

Finally, she recognizes the house of Doña Provi—the bochinchera—the nosy woman from her old neighborhood who had sold limbers, the cold slushy treats Nelida and her friends had loved in their youth. There had been bochincheras like Doña Provi on every block, old women who knew everything because they spent their days looking out their windows and spying on the neighborhood. Nelida and her friends had never liked the old busybody. All day long she'd sat in her rocking chair on her balcony and watched everyone and everything. Nelida and her friends would each hand over their quarters and receive the sweet mixture served frozen in a plastic Dixie cup. They'd buy their limbers and eat them on the way back to their homes. All of her life, Nelida has had a love of frozen desserts. The bochinchera had never been kind, but her limbers had been good and sweet, and they had contented Nelida until the day she met her husband, the man who gave her a pineapple-flavored piragua from his cart and won her heart and her hand.

The bochinchera's home appears empty when Nelida knocks. The ever-locked gate swings open at her touch. In a rocking chair off to the side of the window sits Doña Provi. Her long black hair is threaded through with silver and she is much older than Nelida ever remembered her being. Her hands are folded in her lap. Nelida greets her, but the bochinchera does not answer. She is dead, and her eyes, which are still fixed on the world outside her window, see nothing and no one.

Nelida crosses the cool, tiled floor to the refrigerator. She opens the freezer door and sees the limbers inside. The clear plastic cups, filled three quarters full with fruit-flavored liquid, are all lined up in rows. Nelida knows which one she wants. She takes the tamarind limber and squeezes the plastic cup slowly, pushing the top of the frozen treat up and over the rim, out and across her waiting tongue, and down into her thirsting mouth.

Muñeca

THERE IS NO air in his in-laws' apartment that he has any right to breathe. Pedro notices the absence of air each evening when he returns home from work. All day long he breathes normally. At work in the mail room with the others—packing and shipping and sorting and labeling in the windowless warehouse-like space—at lunch in the humid grease-laden pizzerias, on the train ride home in the compact airtight metal subway cars, on the Manhattan streets thick with the scent of honey-roasted peanuts cutting through the brisk smoke and exhaust-filled air, he breathes freely and easily, feeling no constriction in his lungs, no obstruction of his air passage. The shortness of breath begins once he makes it back to Brooklyn at the end of each day and turns into his in-laws' building. His breathing grows more and more shallow as he begins the walk down the short hallway. By the time he has made it to the apartment at the hall's end, he is out of breath, winded as though he has just finished running for his life. Just in front of his in-laws' door, the air is close and killing. His breath cannot come fast enough. He tries to pull it from his lungs but it stops short, hovering somewhere in his chest, producing a series of short, jabbing pains. Though he is not an asthmatic, Pedro wishes for an inhaler, a paper bag, an oxygen mask, anything to make the breathing less painful.

There is nothing for it but to knock and hope that someone answers the door. Though he lives here this is not his home. He has no key; his name is on no lease. He and his wife are guests here among his in-laws, newlyweds without a place of their own.

Metal slides away from the peephole; his mother-in-law on the door's other side subjects him to scrutiny. How easily the señora could deny him entry, render him homeless. His wife has no such worries. He is the only one who needs permission to come and go, the only one who must awaken someone to lock the door behind him in the morning and wait for someone to let him in every evening. He doesn't like it when people hold such power over him. All they have to do is refuse to answer the door. He cannot breathe in the face of such daily uncertainty.

HE GREETS HIS mother-in-law with "Buenas" and gets "Hello" in return. Out of politeness, deference, to Rosa who does not speak it, his in-laws save their Spanish for their bedroom, or times when he and his wife are not there. The señora is a small, spare woman. Dressed in a floral shirt, tight-fitting stonewashed jeans, and hi-top Reeboks, she looks to Pedro as if she has not left the house all day, not even to check the mail. Her face, brown as any Indian's is small, with a sharply pointed chin, heavy brows and brightly dark eyes. She steps back to let him pass before she replaces the three deadbolts and safety chain, as fierce about defense and protection as any cacique's wife. Her indifferent greeting powers him through the entrance, past the living room where his wife is sitting and watching television, and straight down the hallway to his wife's old bedroom, the room they now share, the room that has become their home.

His wife scurries behind him, catching him by the arm before he turns the knob. When he turns to her, she lifts her face for a kiss. "Hey," she says. "You're late. Where've you been?"

"Tell you later."

She tugs at his hand and leads him back down the hallway. "Tell me while you eat dinner." When she sees his look, she says, "I was too hungry. I couldn't wait. Don't make that face. I'll keep you company."

Seated at his in-laws' kitchen table, Pedro eats while Rosa sits with him, watching him expectantly. Each night the señora makes two dinners, one for the three of them, and a separate meal for Rosa's ailing father. At least Pedro doesn't have to see him tonight. His father-in-law leaves the bedroom seldom, coming out only for the dinner meal and trips to the bathroom. It is bad enough that Pedro has to come home from work every night and sit down for dinner with his wife's family, feeling like less than nothing. Even feeble and incapacitated, Rosa's father manages to make Pedro know he is nothing but a parasitic worm in someone else's house. At least he does not have to sit directly across from her father tonight and look into the old man's eyes and know that even with his failing kidneys and his weak frame he is still a better provider, that it is Rosa's father and not he himself who is responsible for the roof over their heads, the food on their table, and the toilet paper they use to wipe themselves.

"Good news or bad?" Rosa asks. She reaches out and lays a hand on his arm. Her nails are freshly manicured and he feels a flash of anger at her frivolous spending. He doesn't want to discuss anything in the small open space that bleeds into the living room where his mother-in-law sits watching the end of the movie she and his wife had begun. At his back lies a living room that is immaculately clean, but not at all to his taste. The señora sits back on one of the two large overstuffed couches done in a faded floral print, resting the back of her head against one of the couch's flattened pillows. Her legs nestle beneath a maple-colored coffee table burdened with ceramic elephants. More elephants, with their trunks up for good luck, surround her on the matching end tables at either side of the couch, vying for space with pastel-colored lamps and shell-shaped vases stuffed full of silk flowers. Pedro keeps his back to all of the good luck, to the room of prosperity. The plate before him sits atop a thick plastic placemat bearing pictures of oversized fruit. Whenever he lifts his fork or glass, bulbous pears and clusters of grapes look back at him. In his own house, he will insist on doilies with edges as delicate as the mundillo lace made back home. Thinking of his future home allows him to take a deep breath in the airtight apartment of his in-laws. In his own home, he will insist that Rosa serve the right foods—bacalao, sancocho, alcapurrias, pernil—not baked chicken, green beans, and mashed potatoes. Thinking of future meals allows him to eat with relish as he lowers his head to his plate and fills his mouth with food he has not worked to pay for, food his wife has not cooked, food that has been prepared for him by his wife's mother to whom he is already beholden.

He slices a piece of chicken and runs it through his mound of mashed potatoes, shoveling it all into his mouth before answering. "I applied for a place today," he says. "I got us on the list for a two-bedroom over in East New York on Miller, between Pitkin and Glenmore. It's by the A train, across the street from the Van Siclen stop. I'll be able to take one train to work and I won't have to make any switches."

"Two bedrooms?" she asks. "How did you manage that?"

"I told them you were pregnant."

At her protest, Pedro lifts a finger to his lips. "Shh." A smile softens his face. "Before we move, we'll make it true."

Move. As soon as he says the word aloud, his chest loosens and his lungs fill with air. Yes, they would move from this home that was not theirs. Living with his wife's parents was no way to spend the first year and a half of their marriage, but they'd had no choice. It certainly had not been his plan when he'd decided to marry her.

THEY HAD FIRST met at a house party in Canarsie. Carefully, Pedro had managed to end up by her side, steadily maneuvering to make it appear unintentional. He knew better than to ask her to dance. He'd seen her rebuff every man who had tried. He drank his beer and sat it on a nearby speaker, taking his time to study her. She reminded him of the women he'd seen back home at church. Covered in their mantillas, silent and observing, these women she reminded him of possessed a stillness all their own, a prepossessing quiet, almost sacred.

He'd tried greeting her first in Spanish, but she'd returned him only an apologetic smile. "I'm sorry," she'd said, "My parents never taught me."

"I asked if you came with your friends."

"Just one. Marilena." She looked around, briefly searching. "She's here somewhere."

"She didn't leave you?"

"Of course not," she said. "She wouldn't do that."

"My friend Ismael invited me. He told me to come and then he didn't even show up."

"I'm sorry to hear that," she'd said.

"Some friends!" Pedro said. "They've left us on our own and we don't even know anybody."

"Now we can say we know each other," Rosa said.

Pedro picked up his beer and moved closer to her, as close as he dared, close enough to inhale the perfume of her. He flashed her his most charming grin. "So true."

Once he introduced himself, he'd found her eager for conversation, grateful to be acknowledged. Each man she'd turned down for a dance had immediately hied off to the kitchen for a drink, or retreated to the far side of the room. None had lingered to talk. He later learned the reason behind her aloofness—she could not dance—but that night, he'd found her coolness refreshing in a room full of sweaty work-worn bodies, her silence charming in a living room filled with chatter and noise. He looked at her and saw a future. He wasn't a man for pointless courtship, dating until something better came along. He had everything he needed, except a woman to look after him and children to look up to him. Maybe it had been the beer talking, but he'd figured she'd be grateful if he offered her a chance to spend her life with him and privileged her to bear his children. He had come from a family of women, growing up with three older sisters, and if he knew anything, Pedro knew that when it came down to it, marriage and children were what women all wanted, despite their penchant to pretend otherwise. Even the ones who talked about careers and respect, partnership and support, goals and financial security, fretted and longed for marriage and children once they'd accomplished all of the other goals on their lists. Not only did they want it, but they had specifications as well. They wanted it before they reached a certain age, before they were the last single woman in their group of friends, before the firmness of their thighs gave way to dimpled flesh. Rosa was young still—barely nineteen—but he could save her from all such needless worry. Surely, she would thank him for finding her and saving her from wasting time. Yes, she would be grateful.

If only she had stayed that way.

Once married, she'd watched him with questioning eyes, wondering why he couldn't support her in a better fashion, why they had to live with her parents, when things would change so they could have an adult life. All of his promises for a better life had gone up in smoke. Timing had worked against him, making his best-laid plans go awry. He'd fallen prey to a housing scam and had been pushed out of his apartment. Shortly after, his hours at work had been cut. He'd had to marry her cheaply, in a courthouse, and move right in with her folks afterward. At first she was as anxious as he to get out of her parents' home, but as days turned to weeks and weeks slid into months, his wife settled back into being her parents' daughter and Pedro began to feel more like a live-in boyfriend than anyone's husband.

Pedro swallows the last forkful of chicken and tries to remember that he'd started this meal smiling.

She pats his hand. "I have good news too. There's a surprise in the bedroom." When the look on his face turns lustful she says, "Not that kind of surprise."

As soon as Pedro enters their bedroom, he sees a large mahogany armoire standing against the wall where his wife's dresser has stood for so long. To make room, the dresser has been moved to the corner closest to his wife's bed. "What do you think?" she asks.

When he doesn't answer, she opens one of the armoire's tall heavy doors. "Look," Rosa says, gesturing like a game show hostess to show off Pedro's shirts hanging neatly, suspended from a metal rod, their hems and cuffs swaying. "My parents wanted us to have this," she says, rubbing her hand along the armoire's side. It is a beautiful piece of furniture, a deep burnished mahogany with a natural shine, heavy and solid without a scratch. Taller than any man, it looks expensive, looming above him, its two front door panels ornately carved with scrollwork. Next to the armoire, he feels inconsequential, small.

"They've given us enough," he says. "Tell them we can't accept it."

The longer he and Rosa stayed, the more the gifts piled up, lying in wait for whenever they could afford to make the move. His in-laws expected them to take Rosa's old bed with them when they moved, but Pedro didn't want to spend the rest of his life surrounded by the remnants of his wife's childhood. It was bad enough that she still had posters of Menudo, New Edition, and Prince taped to her bedroom walls. When they'd returned from their courthouse wedding, his mother-in-law had presented them with a set of good china and a set of crisp white sheets for their new home, guilting him into acceptance by saying, "It would have been a wedding present if you'd had a ceremony and reception."

"Now we won't have to buy a dresser," Rosa says.

"You're saying I can't afford it?"

"Isn't it good to save where we can?"

Beneath the harsh glare of the overhead light, the wood's finish glowed out of place, making Pedro think of thick, sumptuous carpets, papered walls, butlers, and chandeliers. It would never fit in with the small two-bedroom rent-controlled apartment he was seeking; bringing it in would make any place he could afford look like a dump. "*We?* How can you save something you don't have? What money do you bring in? All you do is watch television all day or go to the salons for perms and manicures. We could save a lot more if you kept your ass at home."

"My mother already does everything here." Rosa sits back on her girlhood bed, leaning back on her elbows, unbothered.

Pedro pushes at the armoire, but it won't budge. "Everyone does something in this house but you and your father."

"He's sick," she says. "That has nothing to do with any of this."

Pedro balls his hand into a fist and punches the side of the armoire, liking the feeling enough to repeat it.

"Stop!" she cries. "You'll ruin it."

"'It has nothing to do with you, Pedro,'" he mocks, making his voice shrill. "Neither does this stupid piece of furniture," he says, kicking it. "'Don't Pedro! You'll ruin it. Then my life will be over when I don't get what I want!' 'Don't ruin it! It's just a piece of wood after all. It's not a man!' You and your parents and their hand-me-downs. Mami and Papi will give little Rosa whatever she wants. Fuck Pedro! He ain't nobody. His opinion ain't shit! He don't even pay rent." When he tires of abusing the armoire, he turns and faces her. "You think I can't see the way they look at me? Like they're wondering what kind of guy they let into the family."

"My parents love you," Rosa says, rising on the bed, balancing on her knees. She tries to grab his arm. "You're being ridiculous!"

"Ridiculous? You think I don't know what they're probably saying? Poor Rosa. Married to that bum. He promised her the world and she's still at home with us. Twenty years old and her life's already crap. Don't bother to deny it," he tells her.

She doesn't.

A knock sounds on the bedroom door. The señora's voice calls, "Is everything okay? I heard a noise."

Pedro whispers to Rosa, "Answer her." His wife stands frozen. He turns to the door and looks around the room for an alibi. "Everything's fine," he says. "I was just moving the new dresser you gave us around to make more room."

There is silence on the other side of the door. He imagines his mother-in-law with her ear pressed against it, eavesdropping. Then the señora asks, "You like it? Very nice, no?"

"Very nice," he answers.

Pedro waits a few minutes, until he is sure the señora has returned to her movie in the living room. He comes to stand near the bed, positioning himself between his wife and the door. "Why didn't you say something?" he hisses.

"She knew everything was fine."

"Easy for you to say. They're your parents. They're not breathing down your neck, following your every move, eavesdropping on your every word. She's just itching for any excuse. Do you see how fast she came running? The sooner we get out of here and into our own place, the better."

"You didn't have to hit it," Rosa complains. "It's just as good as new."

"Only new is as good as new. You don't see me bringing my stuff in here. I got rid of it so we can start brand new, but you want us to have a house full of ramshackle stuff. That's what you want, right?" he asks. "Don't you want—w-what's that doing there?"

So focused on the armoire, he'd failed to notice the doll sitting atop his wife's dresser. A typical gift shop doll—the kind one finds in gift shops all over the Caribbean—the plastic woman wears a wide straw skirt and balances a woven basket full of plastic fruit on her head. Knowing eyes below a multicolored scarf stare back at Pedro. The doll, dressed in a lacy yellow short-sleeved top, holds her brown arms straight out to Pedro, beckoning him.

As if glad to change the subject, Rosa hops off the bed and approaches the dresser. "Marilena dropped it off for me earlier today. She brought back this souvenir from her honeymoon," Rosa says, lifting the doll from the dresser and holding it tenderly. "Look, the eyes open and close." She tilts the doll to show off this feature. When tilted forward, the doll's stiff lashes slide down with a small clicking sound and when tilted backwards, they raise once more. Though the doll's head comes forward, the plastic bananas, pineapples, oranges, strawberries and long oval leaves do not stir. Rosa beams at this, holding the doll reverently. "Isn't she beautiful?"

"Get rid of it," he spits, feeling the doll's eyes upon him.

She rushes to set the doll back on the dresser, as if she fears he might snatch it from her hands.

"What's wrong now?" she asks.

"You're a grown woman. A married woman. You're too old to be playing with dolls. Marilena should know that. I don't know what she was thinking."

"I'm not going to *play* with her," she says, attempting to placate him. "It's a souvenir. I'll just keep her on the dresser."

"I don't want that thing in here," he says.

"It's just a doll." She tries to encircle him in her arms. "What's the big deal?"

"It's looking at me," he says, never taking his eyes off the doll.

"Well, what else am I supposed to do with it?"

Careful to keep his voice pitched low, he says, "The same thing you should have done with all of this other shit! Pack it up and put it away. Look around you." He grabs her jaw and forces her to look where he directs. "Look!"

She pushes against him, but he forces her to look at the armoire, at the posters, at all of her old things. "There's not a damn thing in here that I can say is mine. Not anything here that doesn't remind me that this is your parents' apartment and that this is your room." His voice as tight as a clenched fist, he continues, "This bedroom is full of all your old toys, your old posters. Every night I sleep in this spoiled little girl's room, surrounded by all of your old things. You're a married woman!" With each word, his grip tightens until tears well in her eyes.

"Let me go!"

"Grow up!" He strikes her and she falls back against the bed. It is not until he sees the doll calmly watching him that Pedro realizes what he has done. "Rosa." He fills his voice with apology, but when he reaches for his wife, she scrambles across the bed away from him. She crawls to the farthest corner of the bed and presses herself against the wall. "Don't touch me," she says. She lifts her hand to her face, look-ing from the doll to him in disbelief. In that moment, there are two Pedros. It is as if he is watching himself, like some sort of movie that he has bought a ticket to see. One Pedro moves through the scene; the other Pedro watches to see how it will all unfold. He climbs onto the bed and tries to gather her into his arms. "I didn't mean it," he says.

"I don't care."

He moves back to his side of the bed and waits. He waits for Rosa to get up and run to her parents, but his wife stays where she is, crowded against the far corner of the bed. He waits for his mother-in-law to come rushing and pounding on their bedroom door, but the señora has already gone to bed. He waits for remorse, but no such feeling comes. In the midst of all this waiting, he makes himself comfortable enough to sleep through the night. He turns away from his wife who is ignoring him and finds himself facing the dresser, eye to eye with the observant doll. Her arms, held straight out, reach for him. He squeezes his eyes shut and tries to summon his earlier feeling of happiness, tries to imagine what his new apartment will look like. Eyes closed, he works to picture himself in his brand-new bedroom, surrounded by his own four walls, but all he can see are the open and unblinking eyes of the nearby doll.

HIS SISTERS—Carmen, Pilar, and Leticia—had painted his face and called him *muñeca*, doll-baby.

They came for him once the house emptied of adults and the odds were in their favor. Two, four, and six years older than him, they pooled their weight, their height, their weapons and their anger, using them all to overpower.

"Muñeca!" they called, pulling him from his hiding place in the closet. "Go get Mami's doll," they told him. "We want to play with it."

"Get it yourself," he said.

"See this?" Pilar asked, showing him their father's leather belt. "Now get the doll!"

"No!"

Leather licked his leg. Pilar readied the belt for another lash, cracking it this time against his back. "Now get it," she said. "Before I make it hurt."

He entered his parents' room slowly, as if expecting to be caught at any moment. Their room was always off limits, the tall white door remaining closed at all times. He'd hidden in there a few times, believing his sisters would not disturb him, but they had found him anyway, lying flat on the floor beneath the bed with its fluffy white coverlet. On the wall opposite his parents' bed, the bureau spread out, a wide thing, as if it had wings. In its center, propped against the thick mirror and under the canopy of his mother's dried and withered bouquet, sat the doll his sisters wanted. It was not a doll for play but the bridal doll that had been used at his parents' wedding. Dressed in a gown identical to the one his mother had been married in, the doll was meant to be a miniature replica of the bride. The bosomless doll wore a heavy wedding dress that had once been white but had now yellowed in splotches and faded to a dull ivory. A vee of lace joined at her collar and came straight down her center, another vee of lace circled her middle, and two more trimmed the cuffs of her long splotchy sleeves. The doll sat with her back against the mirror, her legs sticking straight out in front of her, her arms down at her sides. A short veil, secured on either side of her ear with a fake seed pearl, covered her dark hair. A fringe of straight cut bangs framed the painted brown eyes topped by dark swirls meant to convey long lashes. The doll's nose was smaller, slimmer, and straighter than any of their own, the mouth a small closed bud framed by two red circles of blush. Older than his oldest sister, Leti, the doll had been sitting that way for some fourteen years, undisturbed. No one was to touch the doll and well his sisters knew it.

"Go ahead. What are you waiting for?" Carmen and Leti were on either side of him and Pilar still held the belt.

"Pick it up," Pilar said.

In his hands, the doll's dress of fake satin was sticky with age and time, her lace a dull dirty white, her face covered in fine dust. With her glazed porcelain face white as an egg, she looked nothing like his mother. Her dress bore pinpricks from where wedding guests had once pinned dollars in homage to the bride.

"Let's cut her hair," Carmen said.

"Mami will know," Leticia warned.

"We can give her just a trim," Pilar suggested.

"No," Leti said, "Let's do something else."

They leapt at him all at once. Carmen and Pilar pushed him down onto the lowered toilet lid—their short ragged nails digging, their fingers bruising—then draped a towel around his neck and held his arms at his sides while Leti closed in with a pair of shears.

When he tried to fight back, Pilar popped him to make him sit still, delivering stinging blows to his ears, arms, and legs with the back end of a white enameled hairbrush. None of his sisters ever used that brush on their own hair. Its round, wide white base featured the picture of a cat that had been drawn to look like a girl. Dressed in a jumper, the cat-girl sported a bow between her feline ears and gazed at herself in a handheld mirror. That brush—whose soft bending bristles would give way beneath the coarseness of his sisters' unyielding hair—was reserved for the lifeless cornsilk hair of his sisters' dolls. Now they wielded it against him.

Leti poured water onto his head and combed his wet hair down. She cut quickly across the front of his hair, giving him lopsided, jagged bangs. Hair cuttings fell into his eyes, settling onto his lips, itching at the back of his neck. Then she got the makeup and went to work on his face. Eyeing him as if she were Picasso and he her latest masterpiece, standing near him then stepping back from where he was seated, with one sister on either side of him, she held his struggling, squirming body in the chair and looked more critically at her handiwork. Finger to the tip of her chin, dissatisfied, she returned to her canvas, tweaking until she had gotten it right. "There," she said when she was done.

Finally released, he dashed to the bathroom's mirror and saw that they'd made him look like a girl, painted his eyelids with deep blue eye shadow, stenciled an exaggerated mouth over the lines of his own lips and filled it in with greasy red lipstick, rouging in two bright pink dots of blush high on the apples of his cheeks. Pilar had punched at his face with their mother's mascara brush to give him something she called a beauty mark, a large black dot above his upper lip, a fake mole.

Standing behind him, they laughed and blew kisses. "Don't you look so pretty?" Carmen said.

"You did a great job," Pilar told Leti.

Leti brought the bridal doll to the mirror, held it up alongside Pedro's face and said, "You two could be sisters."

Pedro lashed out, his flailing arm cuffing Leti's face and sending the bridal doll flying across the bathroom. The doll landed between the tub and toilet, her head loose on her neck. One of the seed pearls fell off her veil and rolled under the sink. Pedro forgot about fighting once he saw the ruined doll. There would be no way to restore her appearance or tell how she had reached her disheveled state without revealing what had taken place. Disgust would trump pity and his father would say, "Your *sisters*? You *let* your sisters do this to you?" No, he could never tell.

IN THE MORNING Pedro awakens from a fitful sleep, dirty and rumpled, having slept in yesterday's work clothing. He has not left the bed since he'd climbed in it after Rosa, for fear that if he showered and changed, he might return to their bedroom and find her gone. He awakens to find his wife on the far side of the bed, huddled away from him. Though she hasn't looked at him all night or said a word to him, her presence says it all. He pulls her by the waist back up against him.

"No," she moans, trying to scoot away. "Leave me alone."

Saying nothing, he turns her flat on her back and gazes upon her face. She looks at him, eyes accusing and wounded. "Let me see," he says.

"Don't touch me," she whispers.

"Let me see," he repeats.

She tenses the minute he touches her and holds perfectly still. The bruise is dark and her cheek slightly swollen. The bruising is noticeable, but not incredibly so. He looks at it critically and ignores the haggardness that has come into her face overnight, looks past the fear that has never before been in her eyes. He pats the mark with the fleshy pads of his index and middle fingers. When she winces, he says only, "Makeup should hide it. Fix your face and cover that up before your parents see what you made me do." He says it casually, as if he is a friend offering advice, as if it is her fault. Then he gets out of the bed and comes face to face with the watchful doll.

"Don't forget what I said about that thing," he says, expecting no more protests. Keeping his eyes on the doll, he gathers his shower things and chooses his clothing for the day. Bent over the top right-hand drawer, he is annoyed to still feel the doll's eyes upon him. Who is she to watch his every move as he goes about his day? Casually, nonchalantly, Pedro raises his hand as if to adjust his wife's perfume bottle, and—reaching out—lets fly his hand, sending the observant doll crashing to the floor.

Gathering his shower things happily now, he breathes easier and more deeply. Stepping over the doll on his way out of the bedroom, Pedro looks down and sees that she has fallen on her back, arms beckoning and eyes wide open, staring straight ahead.

How to Make Flan

I WAS SETTLED in for the evening, comfortably watching early evening game shows when my father called. "Come home," he said.

"How're you doing?" I asked, pretending as if hearing from him were not a rare, rare thing. For the last four years, I'd been living in West Philadelphia in a converted Victorian house on a quiet tree-lined street just blocks away from campus. I had not seen my father in all this time.

"How soon can you come?"

I looked at the books stacked on my coffee table. Most were over-due at the library. A few had been recalled. I had been meaning to start my paper for the last few hours but had somehow managed to postpone it in favor of dinner and *Jeopardy!* I was only two and a half hours from home, but I thought of my poverty, my debt, and my courses, and made excuses. I reminded my father that this was the fall semester of my last year at Penn, a delicate time. I told him I was in the middle of writing a paper. That I couldn't afford it. That I had enough credit-card debt to make a grown man cry. That I had neither the time nor the money to come to Brooklyn right now. I ended with, "It was good of you to call."

"Not so good," he said.

"Is something wrong?"

"Your abuela is in the hospital."

"Why didn't you tell me?"

"I just did. That's why I called. She wants to see you."

"Is she okay? I mean, what's wrong with her?"

He said, "Everything."

The Final Jeopardy subject was Twentieth-Century U.S. Presidents. Alex Trebek asked the contestants to make their wagers. This could be a trick, I thought. Only I couldn't guess why my father would want to see me so badly that he'd resort to this. I would not come back home for him, but I would for Abuela and he knew it. My father moved back in with Abuela once my parents divorced. Had it not been for that, I would have seen more of her. I listened as my father predicted she wouldn't recover. I promised to see them in the morning as Alex asked the contestants to name the only president whose first middle and last name all had the same number of letters. *Who is Ronald Wilson Reagan?* I silently guessed. I lifted the shade of my window and looked out onto my front porch, idly watching the brittle leaves pile up on the railings. The wind was swirling them, lifting them, hinting at snow.

DESPONDENT SECURITY GUARDS nod as I walk past them. Receptionists don't even lift their heads from the latest magazines. No one asks me for ID or makes me sign in. I find my own way down hallways painted in muted colors and retro designs.

I hear my father's voice as I near Abuela's hospital room. "Mami, try to be reasonable."

"But I don't want a TV. Why do you come here to bother me?"

Abuela is swathed from neck to toe in layers of thick white cotton sheets topped by a beige blanket. She looks as if she is being prepared for burial. My father sits by her side, looking older than he did when I saw him last.

"Dios mio, who is this?" she asks. "You did this for me. You are my favorite son."

"Mami, I'm your only son," he says.

When she smiles, I see that her face is frozen on one side. The left side of her smile slides downwards into a frown. When she talks, only one side of her face moves. "Nieta," she murmurs, "Ven acá."

Abuela struggles to sit up, stretches out a hand to me. I can't help but think that this woman is not Abuela; that someone has switched her with a bad fake. Abuela chases people with wooden spoons and smacks them hard on their hands. She bangs pots and pans. She is always standing, always on her feet.

Her hospital bed is the old-fashioned kind with a crank at the foot of the bed to raise or lower it. It is closer to the window than it should be. I walk to the head of it and press her hand to my lips, kissing the paper-thin skin. "How's my abuelita?" I ask. "How are you feeling?"

"Like a prisoner," she says and then bursts into a fit of coughing. A nurse, standing just outside the door runs in with water. Soon Abuela settles down. She sits up against her pillows, stronger and more alert.

"Mami, be careful," my father says, holding her arm.

"Are you okay?" I ask.

She tries to shake my father off. "They're just trying to impress you. They won't even give me water when I ask for it, only when they want me to have it. I can't drink when I'm thirsty and when I'm not they try to drown me."

"They have their reasons," my father says.

She curses in Spanish and my father rises from his seat. This is more like her.

"Mami!"

She waves him off. "You can go now. I just want my nieta. Wait outside."

Once he is gone, she says. "I missed you. Why did you stay away so long?"

Before I can answer, she says, "Men and women divorce, not families."

"I'm sorry. I—"

"It's okay," she says. "You're here now. My nieta. You've grown so beautiful." Then she motions me closer. "They won't let me go home.

I tell them I'm fine and they say 'Let's see'. These doctors are crazy. Do you understand that?" she asks.

"Maybe they want to make sure you're one hundred percent," I say, not wanting to take sides.

"How can I get better in here? The food they feed me is not fit for a pig." She grabs my hand and tugs me down so I am looking into her eyes. They are cloudy, the irises milky gray; her left eye threatens to close. She searches my face. "I want you to bring me something. Will you?"

"What did the doctors say?"

"Do you think I listen to crazies?" she asks. Although we are the only ones in the room, she pulls me down even closer to her and whispers, "Nieta, I want you to make me some flan."

"I don't think the doctors would want you to have anything they haven't given you," I say.

"Flan is not going to kill anybody," she says.

I shake my head to let her know I mean business, but she doesn't let go of my hand.

"I want some flan," she says. "You remember I used to make it for you when you were sick?"

"I remember."

"You don't want to deny my last wish?"

"Don't talk like that," I say. "Trying to give me a guilt trip won't work."

"No guilt trip," Abuela says. "Blackmail. You owe me." She turns onto her side and pulls the cover over her thin shoulder. "You can go now too."

"WHAT DID SHE WANT?" My father is waiting for me when I leave the hospital room. He takes my bag and hefts it over his shoulder. "She wants you to bring her something, doesn't she?"

"Just to talk."

As soon as we leave the hospital, he lights up. We walk to the subway together and he fills me in. He has a new job, higher pay and more responsibility. He has been dating a woman from Panama, but she is more serious than he is.

He hands me a token and we go through our separate turnstiles and go down the stairs for the local. "How's school?"

"It's fine," I say. "We're about to go into finals."

He nods, flicks his cigarette onto the tracks. "How is your mother?" my father asks.

"I haven't seen her yet. I came straight to the hospital."

My father nods. He says, "The train is coming," and this closes the conversation.

Something I never could understand, my parents. Two workaholics. They loved their jobs more than anything else. Including each other. Including me.

I remember Abuela yelling at them to slow down. She once told me, "All of this money and hard work, but your parents are missing out on the most important thing."

"What's that?" I had asked her.

"You," she said.

So busy working toward the next promotion, putting in overtime, going in on holidays and weekends to build up their time, they couldn't have a marriage, let alone raise a daughter. So they got divorced and I went to boarding school.

I get on the train. He doesn't. He will catch the express on the upper level. "Say hello to your mother for me," my father says as the silver doors close between us.

MY MOTHER IS in the kitchen making her lunch for work when I let myself in.

"So how is she doing?" she asks.

I hang my coat in the hallway closet and drop my bag onto a couch. "She's fine."

"How does she look?"

I join her in the kitchen and kiss her cheek out of habit. "Fine."

My mother mixes tuna fish with mayonnaise in a plastic bowl.

"Fine? Is that how they teach you to talk at that Ivy League school? I'm paying all this money for 'fine?'"

"She doesn't like the food in there."

"Who could blame her?" My mother spoons tuna fish onto bread and makes two sandwiches.

"Dad doesn't think she's coming back out."

She drops the spoon and bowl into the sink and begins to wash them, shaking her head sadly. "What a thing for him to tell someone. God, I hope that's not true. She's always been good to us. You especially."

"She threatened me."

"With what?"

"She wants me to make her some flan and sneak it in to her."

"She knows she can't have that. And you know you can't make her that stuff. It's way too rich. She should know better. Don't even think about it," my mother says, as if her opinion is one that carries weight.

"Dad asked how you were. He said hi," I tell her. She pretends not to hear me. She ziplocks her sandwiches into bags and slides them into a lunch bag that can keep food hot or cold, depending.

"The next time you see her, give her my love."

I DROP MY stuff off in my room. I barely recognize it. My mother has taken my posters down and has mounted all of my academic awards on the walls. She has taken my books off the shelves and replaced them with row upon row of my old dolls. Bald-headed Barbies lean against the shelves, Kens with their hands and feet bitten and disfigured and Skippers without heads preen on the shelves, sit, pose, and lean into one another. Plastic hands that I had slowly chewed on while waiting for my mother to come home from working overtime. Blonde cornsilk strands of hair that I had pulled out one by one each time she broke a promise. Heads that I had popped off when I had finally had enough for a time. The dolls were my mother's way of assuaging guilt. Every time she took on another shift, worked more hours than she was scheduled to, stayed at work rather than come home on holidays and weekends, she brought me an eleven-and-a-half-inch Barbie doll that I had not asked for. They were supposed to make me feel better about not seeing her. As I pull on my pajamas, I remind myself that I am an adult now, that I have matured. I resist the urge to twist Ken's plastic head off and I try to get some sleep.

MY FATHER AND grandmother are arguing when I get there the next day.

They stop when they see me. "Look who's here," my father says.

I ask, "How are you feeling, Abuelita?"

"Not so good."

"What's wrong?"

"Tengo más hambre que maestra de escuela," she says. Then she looks at me. "You don't understand me?"

I tell her that I stopped taking Spanish after my sophomore year. She rolls her eyes in disgust. "This is your child," she says to my father.

My father explains, "She said she's hungry."

"As hungry as a schoolteacher," Abuela adds. "But I'd be better if your father here would stop trying to make me eat."

The table by her right arm can be wheeled closer or further for her convenience. On it is a Styrofoam cup of flat ginger ale, a small ramekin of pudding, and a clear container of fruit salad. Chunks of watermelon and pineapple sit in their own juices.

"But Mami, you know what the doctors said. You have to eat. You have to build up your strength," my father says. "You're too weak."

Abuela waves him off. "Ya, mijo. Ya ya. Déjame en paz. I'd have to be a pig to eat the food they give me here. You know that I can't eat that stuff. It makes me go to the bathroom."

He says, "You'll never get better that way."

Abuela looks at me like a supplicant. "It's so greasy. Who could eat it?"

"Mami, it's not that bad," my father says.

Abuela's hand comes down on her tray. "You like it so much you can eat it!" She knocks over the ginger ale.

My father grabs tissues and kneels to clean up the mess. He apologizes, "She's been like this since she got here. She won't listen."

"Am I dead yet? I still have ears," she says.

"What's wrong with your food?" I ask.

"That fruit is older than I am," she says.

"What about the pudding?"

She looks at it suspiciously.

"Want to try it?"

"Maybe a little bit."

My father throws his hands up. "I just tried to get you to eat that!"

"You're not my nieta," Abuela says, a crafty smile on her face. "Give me the slop. I'll taste it."

She tries to hold her cup with her bad hand, but she cannot steady it. The ramekin wobbles. Each time she dips her good hand with the spoon into the container, the yellowish pudding slides out.

"Here, Abuela, let me," I say as I take the ramekin from her.

I spoon the pudding out for her and feed it to her. She is like a greedy child, gobbling every bit I give her as my father watches, unspeaking.

"How is that?"

"It's slop, but it's better than nothing," she says. She tries to grab my wrist with her weak left hand. "That's enough. Thank you."

"You've got to keep your strength up," I tell her.

"We don't want to lose you," my father says.

She makes a face at him. "I'm not going anywhere."

I GO HOME with him to find her comb and brush. We don't talk about my mother.

In my grandmother's house are many candles, knick knacks, and saints. She has tried to cram a whole island into her overcrowded apartment. Elephants march across the coffee table, trunks up. Coasters bear the faces of parrots and coquis. Large wooden spoons in three different sizes hang from the wall in the kitchen. A green can of soda crackers sits on a counter and I know it is filled to the brim with rice, not crackers. A pilón, mortar and pestle, wait above the refrigerator for her to come home and mash cooked green plantains with fresh garlic to make mofongo. A large aluminum pot with its blackened bottom sits on the back burner of the stove, ever ready.

My father takes me to her bedroom and opens her door, leaving me to find the comb and brush. Everything is just as I remembered it. Over her bedroom door, a palm leaf is twisted into the shape of a cross. It will remain there until next Palm Sunday. A bust of Jesus adorns the end table in her bedroom. Four near-empty bottles of prescription medicine sit on her dresser. Next to them lie her brush and comb, still filled with long strands of her hair. I see Abuela here, vital and alive, dusting off her dresser mirror, allowing me to help brush her hair, showing me which of her medicines thinned her blood, kept her blood pressure down, or helped her to breathe and which ones protected her from all the other ones. Her bedroom is a walking botanical. Scientific medicine jostles for space with Santería concoctions, Catholic remedies and vials of holy water and holy oil are lined up next to health food store medicines in clear plastic pouches. These medicines were toys to me when I was younger, things to be suspicious of when I was older and forewarned by my mother and others who didn't believe in that stuff, things to make fun of once I went to college and learned to know better. Now as I look at them, I just see an old woman's attempts to prolong her life as creatively as she could.

THE NEXT DAY she is arguing with my father over the television in her room.

"It's wasting your money, I don't need it."

"But Mami, you might change your mind. You might want to watch some shows."

"I've seen enough Phil Donahue and Jerry Springer to last my whole life."

"How about if I just turn it on so you can see what there is to watch?"

"Do you think I want to be watching things that aren't real?"

"Mami, just look at—"

"Leave it!"

My father moved to turn the TV on. "Just see—"

"Get out of here! No me molestes!"

"But Mami—"

"I don't want to see your face any more. Go!"

My father walks to the door slowly as if waiting for her to call him back. She pretends he is already gone. She pats the bed and I go to her. "Did you bring me what I asked for?"

"Not exactly."

She makes a face at me. "But I did bring your comb and brush, Abuela."

"Okay," she nods. "But tomorrow, I want flan. Is your father standing outside my door?"

Now he is my father, not her son. I go and check. The hallway is clear. "No. He's gone."

"Good."

"He was just trying to help," I say. Sitting on the edge of her bed with a comb and brush, I work out the snarls and kinks in Abuela's hair.

"Help me put my foot in the grave!"

"Don't you think you're being a little harsh on him?" I ask. "He loves you."

"I know," she says, breathing like it's hurting her. "I love him too. No mother ever loved a son more, but he's killing me." She looks at me, imploring. "I don't want to be here. I don't want to eat that food. I want to go home and be in my own bed. I don't want to die here."

"Don't say that." Something in me trembles. "You're not going to die. Remember what you said? You're not going anywhere?"

Tears slip from her eyes. "Tell that to my son. Every time I look into his eyes, I see death looking back at me."

"Abuela." I take her hand. She doesn't look good. If at all possible, she seems smaller and weaker than a moment ago.

"No more talk about that," she says. Her face brightens momentarily. "Tell me about your school and Philadelphia."

I have been happy and comfortable away in Philadelphia. I tell her about Clark Park and the Farmer's Market. I tell her what it's like to have a porch instead of a stoop. I try to explain the difference between a water ice and an Italian ice.

"I would like to visit you," she says.

"Anytime," I say, glad to talk of her getting better. "But I'll have to clean up first."

She laughs and falls into a fit of coughing that lasts too long. Her cough rattles in her chest and leaves her spent. She won't let me call the nurse. I offer her water. I hold her hand. I wish for my father to come back and take over.

"Let me get someone."

The hand that I am holding tightens on mine with surprising strength. Her hands squeeze but I don't pull away. "No me dejas," she says. *Don't leave me.* It's easy for me to forget how sick she has always been when I hear her arguing and yelling. She's been this way for so long that sometimes I take it for granted. Her voice trembles and she squeezes my hand harder and harder. I have never seen her afraid.

"No," I say. I swallow hard. "I won't leave you."

I have no idea how long it takes before her breathing has calmed. Too long. Finally, she looks at me and pats my hand, smiling weakly. "Tell me, nieta, would I like Philadelphia?"

"You would," I tell her. When I say this, I am thinking of the vegetable stands between Chestnut and Locust. The large white trucks the Senegalese men drive, the rickety wooden stalls they erect to sell their fresh vegetables. The long snaking lines of people crowded onto the curb and spilling out into the street, thumping melons and inspecting yams, arguing over the price of overripe produce. I remember Abuela taking me to market and inspecting mangoes, avocados, guavas and breadfruits, arguing with the vendors and loving every minute of it.

She wants me to continue to brush her hair. I scratch out the tiny white flakes of dandruff that nurses have ignored, pulling her long hair out from behind her and brushing it all the way down to the straggly ends. Each stroke relaxes her a little more, making her sleepy, just like it used to. Yawning, she says, "My hair is from Spain and my face is from Africa. And you nieta, you look just like me."

I laugh at our old joke. When I was younger, I didn't know who or what I was. I had a black mother and a Puerto Rican father, and I didn't know what that made me. By fourth grade I had learned that in this country, it was neither possible nor desirable to be both. Kids teased me, calling me "elstupido." Girls pulled my hair, wondering if it was a weave. Grown men approached me in Spanish on my way to or from school, angry when I didn't answer because I couldn't understand. There were two sides of me and one of them was always getting in trouble. My mother blamed the Puerto Rican side of me and my father blamed the black side.

I don't remember what caused it, but I came to my grandmother in tears one afternoon, asking, "Abuela, what am I?"

She didn't ask me what happened. She just shook her head at me. "Don't you know who you are?" She laced her fingers through mine. "You are my granddaughter, my nieta. You are everybody's daughter. You are the conquistador, the Indian, and the slave, struggling to be one. You are three kings bringing gifts. You are a fortress. You are chains and shackles. You are the ocean. And the sand beneath the waves. You are the pride of the sea. You are the breeze that blows from the shore. You are my granddaughter, my nieta. You are me, nena. You are me."

As my grandmother drifts off to sleep, I pull the comb through her hair and think of how much I still need her. I want to lie down beside her on her hospital bed. I want her to wrap her arms around me. I want her to give me all her answers.

I FIND MY mother and father necking on the couch. One shame-faced, the other daring, they partly detach, long enough for my father to help my mother sit up. Long enough for her to smooth her skirt, blow hair out of her eyes. Long enough for him to drape his arm over her shoulder and leave it there.

"Will I see you tomorrow?" I ask him before either of them can speak.

He shrugs. "What difference does it make? She only wants her nieta," he mocks, sounding like a small child.

Once he has gone, my mother tries to explain. "He told me what happened. He said he didn't know where else to go."

"So he came here?" I can't keep the sarcasm from my voice. "After not stepping foot in this apartment since I was what—twelve—he decides to drop by today?"

"It was the one place he knew he wouldn't have to face you." Suddenly, miraculously, my mother has become an expert on my father. Suddenly, she knows so much.

"Except here I am."

"We kind of lost track of time."

"I see," I say, although I don't.

"He was very hurt. He pouts when he doesn't get his way," she says. "She threw him out but kept you. He was jealous of you."

"That's ridiculous."

"He's always been like that."

I don't know how he has always been and I don't want to know now. "So am I supposed to be sorry that—"

"No, no. Of course not. He should have understood. You've always been special to her. She was always willing to take you when you were young and your father and I were so busy with everything." She changes the subject. "Do you think she would mind if I came to see her?"

"No," I say. "You should."

"If I could change the past—" my mother begins. She stops, seeming to stare at something in the corner of the kitchen. "We were so young and stupid then. It's a good thing you spent more time with her than us," she says, the closest she will come to an apology.

AS I LAY out the ingredients for the flan, I remember one winter when I was eleven and Abuela made flan to cure my strep throat. She said that the flan would be good for my throat, that it would soothe the soreness and that it wouldn't hurt me to swallow it. Her tiny kitchen was just a rectangle of space sectioned off from the large open living room by a tall counter. I remember the comfort of the living room. From the hi-riser, I could see the back of her, her head and back and shoulders bent over a small saucepan, stirring sugar over a low heat until it caramelized. I could close my eyes and listen to the hushed steps she made in the small square of kitchen space, the sound of metal hitting aluminum as she scraped the clinging bits of caramel from the pan, the crack and spill of eggs, the flourish of water running in the sink to set the mold, the creak of wooden cabinet doors on old iron hinges as she opened the cupboards and pulled out her custard cups, the ping of milk in a glass bowl, all the ingredients of my flan, all of the steps she took to let me know that she was with me and she was making my cure. No matter how high my fever or how dry my throat, the pain all seemed lessened by those safe secure sounds of someone seeking my welfare.

After she'd made the flan and I'd eaten it, she'd settle me once more on the Hi Riser to sleep. She'd brush back the hair from my forehead and lean down to kiss me and I'd feel the dry press of her lips against my hot, feverish skin.

At that moment she'd say, "Te quiero, nieta." *I love you.*

TOMORROW, WHETHER OR not my father decides to show up, I will go and sit with my grandmother.

Tonight I make the flan.

In my mother's kitchen, I pour sugar and a bit of water into a saucepan, stirring it over a low heat until the caramel forms. I pour the caramel out into my mold and set it to the side. I beat eggs until they are frothy. Then I add condensed milk and vanilla, mixing well. Finally, I pour the custard over the caramel. I place my mold inside a larger pan and fill the larger pan partway with water, putting it in the oven to bake.

Tomorrow, my grandmother will be better and stronger than she was today.

Tonight I take my flan from the oven and invert it on a dish. I leave it in the refrigerator overnight and wait for it to take its shape.

Only Son

SO FRAIL THE new, new being. Brown and slick was the thing Nelida could not yet convince herself to call a baby, much less a son. Though not malformed, the tiny living thing seemed unrecognizable. Careful how she held it, Nelida touched, prodded, and inspected the infant, finding nothing that compelled her to love.

Two clean and crisp brown nurses watched nearby. Nelida forced herself to lift the infant. She made a show of cooing at it, making the nonsense noises that set the nurses at ease while she resisted the inner urge to dash the baby to the cold, clean floor. The feeling came upon her suddenly, a gnawing desire as insistent as the cravings had been. Better to end it now, she thought, cradling the infant's tiny neck, resting her thumb against his collarbone.

"What a beautiful sight," her husband said, entering the hospital room. "How are the two of you feeling?"

"Bien," Nelida answered.

"In English," he chided her.

"We feel fine," she said, hating the way her voice sounded around the flat foreign words.

"I heard him cry. His lungs are powerful," he said.

"He's tiny," Nelida said. She thought this one smaller than all the others. How had he managed to escape the graveyard that was her womb? No matter, she would not hope. As soon as she did, his heart would fail and his lungs collapse.

"Tiny but tough," he said, trying to convince the both of them. "You're a natural," he joked, watching the way Nelida held the infant. She had held five babies before Esteban; she knew how it should be done.

"Tomalo," she said, holding the baby away from herself.

"English, Neli."

"Take him!" The gnawing urge resurfaced. She wanted to squeeze the malleable arms, crush the still-soft bones. "Papi, just take him!"

The name flew from her lips before she could call it back.

It began as a cruel joke after they'd lost their third child in a row. Given to him by their neighbors in Rio Piedras, the name was meant to put him in his place, for indeed he was no man's father. They meant it to remind him that he had faults, just like them. They meant it to mask their confusion. For they did not understand why he'd rather take his small cart to the beaches and malls, standing in the hot sun just to sell piraguas to the turistas when he could work at the finca with them. They meant it to humble him, to buckle his knees. But they couldn't make it stick. Couldn't keep the deference from creeping into their tone. They all called him Papi now, forgetting the intended insult, forgetting even his real name.

He pretended not to notice his wife's slip as he held the tiny blinking infant and calculated how many years of saving it would take to bring his family to the States. Mentally, he rearranged their lives. This child was their last chance to leave their mark on this world. He was no longer a young man, but he would do whatever was necessary. He could learn to take orders, work late hours, live poorly, and eat scantily if he could pour out all of the benefits on a son who would grow up to make them proud. Esteban would follow in his footsteps, working for no man but himself. Esteban would listen to his stories and plans and dreams; he would appreciate all that had been sacrificed for him. He would become his partner and one day he'd be able to hand the reins over to his own son, knowing that he was leaving his business in able hands, knowing that everything he'd worked for would continue to grow and thrive. For that, for Esteban, it would be worth it.

"This one will live, Neli. Forget what the doctors say. *No me importa.* I know it. I feel it here," he said, beating one fist against his heart.

"Veremos," Nelida said. *We'll see.*

TWO YEARS OF watching, waiting for the first sign of illness. Nelida steeled herself against Esteban's first smile, his first steps. She was unimpressed that first time he reached up for her and his bright eyes lit on her face with recognition. She was bored with soothing his irritated gums and contorting her face into silly expressions to stop his tears. She was unmoved when she held his warm sated body near to her heart and listened to his lulled breathing like a song unto itself. She wanted more. After two years of uncertainty, of living each day as if it were her child's last—too afraid to look ahead to a future she could not imagine—she became greedy. She could burp a baby in her sleep but wanted to know what it would be like to have her child drink from a cup without help. Her babies did not live long enough to get into everything, to pull things down. She wanted to see her child cry and cling to her on the first day of school, too afraid to leave her. She wanted all of the devotion she had missed. It was little enough to ask. She had paid for it—for him—with five preceding pregnancies.

PUERTO RICAN GIRLS wouldn't give him the time of day unless he gave them something free from his father's store, but black girls found him light skinned and cute. Lying on the bottom bunk in the room his girlfriend shared with two others, Esteban felt momentarily free. Every day after school found him here instead of in the store where his father expected him. With the door closed and secured by the back of a chair, Renay in the crook of his arm and her synthetic braids abrading his cheek, he did not hear the voices of his parents. The freedom would not last, he knew. They were always there, always in his head, calling him, calling him. Right now, he should be helping out in his father's store. Right now, he should be restocking shelves and dusting off the tops of canned goods. Right now, he should be at the register, giving some junkie fifty cents on the dollar for her food stamps so she could score a hit. Right now, he should be playing the role of the good son and making his parents proud.

Instead, he wanted nothing to do with them. Wanted no part of this new life they'd forced upon him. He wanted no part of working downstairs and looking every day into the eyes of men who would switch places with him, men who would gladly trade in their daily jobs to be a merchant's son. The sacrifices meant nothing to him. He was tired of the stories and he didn't want to be here. He wanted Rio Piedras. He wanted Ponce. He wanted Mayaguez. He would even take San Juan, tourist trap that it had become. He would take any of the places where his voice was one among a crowd, its cadence indistinguishable and indistinct. Instead, he was still naked and new. After three years on the mainland, he still felt stripped of his skin.

He heard their voices now. His father reminded him of all the sacrifices they had made for him. His mother reminded him that he was their only son. She pleaded with him to remember all of the children that had gone into making him, all of the Estebans they had lost before he decided to live.

The only thing that could keep the voices at bay was Renay's yielding body. "Let's do something," he said.

"Like what?"

"I don't know. Anything." He pulled her to him and began to kiss her neck.

"Stop." She slapped his hand away.

"Come on."

"Hold on, okay?" She got up from the bed and began to move among the clutter, trying to transform the small bedroom in the small rent-controlled apartment into something else. She lit three sticks of Egyptian Musk, wafting the quick-burning incense in all directions. Then she put a mixed tape of their favorite slow jams into the boom box in the corner.

The voices never said anything new. They were maddening in their repetition, droning insistently. The crooners on the cassette did nothing to drown them out.

"Hit the lights too," he said.

"If I turn the lights out, we won't be able to see anything," she said.

"I don't care."

She flicked the light switch. "Now I can't see."

"You should know where everything is by now," he said. "Just follow the sound of my voice."

When she came to the bed, he tried to pull her beneath him.

"Damn, Esteban, can't you even wait a minute?"

At the sound of his name, the voices whipped themselves into a frenzy. "I told you not to call me that."

"Fine, sorry. Steve. I don't see what the problem is. It's *your* name."

"No it's not," he said. "It's their name."

"They who?"

"Don't worry about it." He reached for her again, but she pushed him away as she leaned over the side of the bed and groped underneath, pulling out an empty box.

"We don't have any left."

He laid back against the pillow. Renay's body would have only stopped the voices for a time, he knew. Shortly after, they would start again, but they would be weaker, like a small insect buzzing beside his ear, needing time to build back to their normal strength. If only he could find a way to free himself of the voices for good. Maybe if he had his own responsibilities, they would leave him alone.

He rubbed her back beneath her shirt and unclasped her bra.

"Come on now," she said. "Stop."

"You already got the lights out and the music on and everything."

"But I told you we're out. You're going to have to go to the store or something."

"That's all right," he said. "I take care of my responsibilities."

Voices calling him home, reminding him, pleading with him, begging him. He fastened himself to Renay, holding her hips tighter, driving into her harder to silence them. What did they know? The voices knew nothing. Nothing at all. Didn't know some nights he could barely breathe even with the window wide open. Didn't know that no one could see him wherever he went because he was just a shadow of the babies his mother had borne before him. Didn't know that speaking English embarrassed him. The voices didn't know he felt caged in all the time by the walls and the buildings, by being spoiled and knowing it, by not being able to deal with the responsibility that came with being the only son. Bearing the weight of his parents' expectations as they drowned him and threatened to pull him under. It was a terrible thing, to live invisibly. A terrible thing to put so much weight on him, enough weight to make him tumble, enough to make him come apart.

DAYS ESTEBAN SPENT watching his son in the apartment above the store while Renay finished high school. Days Nelida spent watching Esteban watching his son, afraid of the restlessness the baby seemed to awaken in him. He complained that the baby was too boring, that the baby slept too much. Whenever he wasn't complaining, Esteban would watch the baby with a hunger too fierce to conceal.

She had given him a bowl of funche to feed little Esteban, but when Nelida went to retrieve it, she found him in the living room—the still-full bowl forgotten on a nearby coffee table—holding his son at eye level, staring into the baby's face as if his gaze could penetrate the infant's flesh.

"He's not going anywhere. He can't even crawl yet," she joked, but Esteban didn't hear. He was whispering something to the baby and when Nelida crept up behind him, she could hear him ask the boy, "Who are you?"

"He's your son," she said. "Why are you talking crazy?"

"I don't think he is. I see so many people in him."

Nelida had been about to suggest he go in for a paternity test when he said, "What's the purpose of having a child if you can't even see your own self in him? He has his mother's skin, your eyes, Papi's nose, and nothing of my own. I keep watching him to see if any of my own features will show up but they never do. He's not mine; he's everyone else's. I can't claim him. I don't see me at all."

"You will in time," Nelida said.

"Mami, when you look at me, what do you see?"

"Don't be a silly. I see you," she said, touching his face. "I see Esteban."

"Esteban," he said. "Of course."

When his mother walked away, Esteban settled the baby on his knee and tried to bounce him. "No wonder you're so heavy."

The baby was not at all like he had expected, and the demands on him did not diminish as he had planned. If anything, his parents used the child to stake deeper claims. Now his father said, "Go to business school. You could turn this store into a chain. You could be rich. You'd have something to hand down to your son. Think of Little Esteban. Think of your son." Now there were expectations from his girlfriend as well, things she wanted, plans she had. She wouldn't hear of him taking the baby to Puerto Rico. "You'll make it so I don't even understand my own son," she said after she caught him talking to the baby in Spanish.

Esteban tried to bounce the baby on his knee, but the baby—carrying the weight of three generations—seemed unbearably heavy, like so much dead weight.

OVER A HEARTY breakfast of café con leche, eggs, and amarillos, Esteban announced, "I'm going to join the army."

"You'll be killed!" Nelida cried.

"There's no war, Mami. Nobody can kill me. It's just regular duty."

"What led to this decision?" Papi asked.

Esteban shrugged. "It's a good deal. They pay for a lot of things."

Papi said, "I can afford business school for you now. Money is no problem for you, my son."

"It's not just the money."

"Then what?"

"You won't understand."

"So you've made your move," Papi said, slicing into a ripe plantain.

"What's that supposed to mean? We're not playing chess."

"No? I've been watching you for months. Do you think I can't see that you're not happy? You think I can't see that you despise everything I stand for? Everything I tried to build, Esteban, I did it for you."

"I didn't ask for any of this."

"What about your son?" Papi asked. "You didn't ask for him either."

"This has nothing to do with him. It's just a few years. He'll be fine here. That way you can make sure I come back," Esteban snapped.

"Look at your poor mother over there. Do you see her?" Papi asked. Nelida had gone to stand by the kitchen counter. She stood there holding a soda cracker tin, removing the lid and replacing it over and over. When Esteban didn't answer, he demanded, "Do you?"

Esteban wouldn't look at her over by the counter, playing with the canister. "You know I do."

Papi rose and pointed at his wife. "But you don't see everything she's done for you! Do you think she wanted to come? I dragged her! I bet you don't even remember the sound of your own mother's tears. Every night for two years she cried to go back home. I had to hold her every night. I even thought she might one day leave me, she hated it here so much. But she didn't. She stayed. She gave it a chance. She dried her tears. For you!"

Esteban rose and shouted, "So when I get out I'll write you both a check!"

The brunt of Papi's hand was like a blur, slapping Esteban hard across the mouth, so hard he bit down on his tongue and tasted blood. They had never chastised their son before. Nelida had to hold him back by the arm. A vein popped out on Papi's head and he no longer looked his age. "Don't you ever say something like that! You disrespect your mother! You say whatever you want to me; I've let you for this long so you're used to it, but that woman cried for you, and if you ever . . ." Papi stopped abruptly, looking at his son as if seeing him for the first time. "What kind of son are you?" he whispered, taking Esteban's face in his hands.

He threw his father's hands off. "The only one you have!" he shouted. "That's right! You wish I was one of the ones that didn't make it. All of us the same, right? All of us Esteban! But we're not. I'm me! How many times did you mix us up, calling *me* with them in mind? You wish one of the other ones had survived instead of me. Well, I'm all you've got and I'm leaving. All this time, you forced me to see your life. What it was like for you. How hard. The prices you paid. Neither of you ever looked at my life. Mami wasn't the only one who didn't want to leave! You never tried to see what it was like for me. You never even saw me. You look at me and you see *them*. You see all the ones before me," Esteban said.

Nelida hugged the green tin and cried. Little Esteban abandoned the yellow truck he'd been pushing across the linoleum during the argument, crawled over to her and tugged the hem of her dress to be picked up. When she didn't respond, he began to cry along with her, "'Buela. 'Buela."

Esteban watched his only son, knowing he could never claim him. He turned to Papi, "I'm your only son," he said. "And I can only be one son. Mami, lo siento." He stepped over his son's yellow truck and walked down the hallway and out of the apartment.

Nelida set the tin on the counter and picked up her grandson to soothe him. At one point, that tin had held the soda crackers it boasted of, but now it was the container she used to hold her uncooked rice. It was a staple in her kitchen, as much a part of it as the wooden spoons hanging above the counter, the large cast-iron caldera sitting on the back burner and the wooden pilón on top of the refrigerator. Never had she thought to see the day when her husband would try to kill her son in her kitchen in front of her rice. So long ago, she was the one who had harbored violent thoughts against him, for which she had been paying since his birth. It was her fault. It was because she had not wanted him to live, because she had wanted to hurt him, because she had not loved him those first few minutes of his life that he had grown into the man he now was. She faced her husband and said, "Look at what you did."

Papi cleared the dishes, pouring café gone cold down the sink's drain. "He's ungrateful."

"You shouldn't have hit him. You shouldn't have yelled."

"He's been spoiled too long. Everybody has to grow up, Nelida."

"He's our only son. When we get too old for this, who will take over? Who will care about all we have done? None of this will mean anything to anyone else. We might as well be back at home with people who know us. He'll leave us. Without him, we'll be all alone."

"We'll have each other," Papi said.

"That's all we ever had."

THAT AFTERNOON, THEY had to keep Little Esteban downstairs in the store with them because their son had not returned. They walked past each other behind the counter without speaking. Nelida brushed past Papi when he was slicing ham for a customer's hero sandwich. She stayed out of his way while she broke open a carton of cigarettes and slowly put up each pack. She handed him change when he needed it, but she did not speak.

"Que oscuro," were the first words she had ever uttered on mainland soil, and her husband had not bothered to correct her. The sky had caught them both by surprise, and Nelida had not been able to find the English words as she stood in front of one of the small windows in the new apartment above their new store, looking up and out at the cloudy darkness trying to push its way into their little bit of space. Fourteen years of scrimping had brought them to a tiny apartment above a corner store across the street from housing projects which squatted below a threatening sky.

That day Nelida had blocked out the sky by reminding herself of all the reasons it was necessary to leave Rio Piedras. They were Puerto Ricans and thus not immigrants but U.S. citizens by right, and Esteban deserved to attend high school and college in the States where he could have the best of everything. That was what Papi reiterated every time she doubted. That was worth leaving behind her Rio Piedras, her home, her sun, her sky. Despite her assurance, that sky which seemed so much darker, so much grayer here on the mainland warned her that she would have to protect herself and her family from it. A sky like that, so dark, could not be trusted. So she gave, turned herself inside out with giving, spread her love and generosity like a mantle over those she held most dear. She gave her husband her livelihood. She gave him six sons although only one survived. She gave her church ten percent of everything she had. She gave her grandson her telenovelas time. She gave and gave and gave; she did not want to give in to her husband, to give up her only son.

All through the day, she kept her silence and her anger. She waited for late afternoon when business always slowed down.

"I have something to say."

"You're speaking to me now?"

"You're the one who's wrong."

"His ingratitude is shameful. *Desgracio.* How am I wrong?"

"You can't be angry at someone for being the way you taught them to be!"

"So I created that monster? I made him speak to us that way and disrespect us so? What does the Bible say? Abraham had only one son, but he was willing to give him up when the Lord asked. He didn't say 'Lord this is my only one and I raised him to think I would always take care of him. Therefore I cannot give him to you.' When it was time to let go, Abraham was willing to do the right thing."

"You are not Abraham!" Nelida said. "And he had other sons with his wife's maid."

"Bastards."

"Stop it! We have only him and you're making him leave! You'd better stop him."

"Should the father beg the son?"

"All these pretty words. All this time I trusted you to speak for us. Now I don't like the things you say. I let you speak and I let you decide. Now I will decide. I want my child. My only son. I let you take me away and bring me here. There's no sound for me here, but I never say a word. I gave you everything. My youth and my heart. I trusted you when you say this was the best for him. All this time I never ask if what you doing was right. I never question. I don't care if you beg. I don't care if you go on your knees. Don't let him leave like this. If you do, he never comes back to us."

He had never heard such a lengthy speech from her in English. And with but few mistakes. "Neli—"

Nelida shook her head when he came toward her. She put up her hands to hold him at bay. "He's my son," she cried, nearly buckling against the counter. She put her hands out to brace herself, to keep herself standing. Her fingerprints smudged the Plexiglas. "He's my son. Mi hijo. Mijo. Mijo. Mi solo hijo, mi ultimo hijo. Mi hijo. Mijo. Mijo."

"He's my son too."

She wrapped her arms around her middle. "Do you remember the day we met?"

"I gave you a free piragua just so you would stand there and eat it while I talked to you."

"Yes," she said. "Piña flavored. If I had known then that God would take all my sons but one and you would drive the last one away, on the day that I met you, I would have let your free piragua melt!"

"Neli, please."

They heard him return. He didn't come through the store but went through the separate entrance straight up to the apartment above.

"You go," Nelida said, wiping her eyes. "You fix it. Make it right or when he goes, I go too."

PAPI KNOCKED ON his son's door and waited for permission to enter, something he'd never before done.

When they came in, Esteban told them, "It's already done. You can't stop me."

"I didn't come to try. Please mijo, may I sit down?"

Esteban shrugged. "It's your house. You don't need to ask me."

Papi sank onto the hard, sloppy bed. Nelida stood by his side. She couldn't picture her son making those sharp tidy beds the way the military men in the movies did. So tight that you could bounce a quarter off the bed. He was too lazy for that type of discipline.

"I wish that you could just hear me," Esteban said.

"I've been hearing you for almost twenty years. You haven't said anything new," Papi said. Nelida pinched his arm. "What I mean is I'm trying to now, my son. Maybe this is the best thing for you now. To go and see the world."

Nelida said, "But please, we want you to come back."

"My son is here."

"Do you think that when you come back, you might go to business school?" Papi asked.

Esteban pulled a pack of cigarettes from his shirt pocket and began to smoke one. He shrugged. "I don't know. Anything is possible. I like making money as much as anybody. I just don't want to be forced."

Nelida watched Papi's shoulders sink. He was so proud, she almost expected him to get up and walk out. "My son, we both didn't say things right earlier this morning. Your mother and I are not a bank. We don't want you to owe us or write a check. We just want you to appreciate how much we love you, my son. So much so that we make mistakes."

Nelida squeezed his shoulder, proud of his effort. She didn't know that it was just the first of many concessions they'd make to their son, didn't know that there was no way to appease him. Nelida willed Esteban to understand that he'd just heard the closest his father would ever come to an apology. Truly, she wasn't even sure he deserved it, but she knew it was their own fault. After struggling so hard to keep him in his infancy, they had lost him as an adult. They had given much to him. Too much. Their love had crippled him, but could they be blamed for loving?

"Hey. I shouldn't have sprung it on you guys like that either. It's not that I don't appreciate. I just want something of my own. If I can make it there, I'll come back and help out. Running this store can't be hard. I was raised in it. It's in my blood. Besides, it's no more trouble than you all taking care of my son till I come back," he said.

Papi leaned back against the headboard. "That sounds good," he said.

"So you will come back home?" Nelida asked, to make sure.

"I can never forget where I came from," Esteban said, finishing his smoke. He cracked the window open to let the air rush in and flicked the clip out the window, watching it sail on a high arc but losing sight of it long before it hit the street below.

A Wish, Like a Candle, Burns

MIGUEL DODGED BETWEEN the two women, a suitcase in each hand, sending Lydia a signal she ignored. This was the third time he'd cut between them when he could have just gone around. Val stepped back, clearing a path for him. Her eyes were hard, glaring, making it clear without words that Lydia could have done better.

Miguel carried the boys' overnight bags. He stopped directly in front of Lydia.

"I'm taking the boys down to the car."

"I just need to say good-bye," she said.

"Isn't that what you've been doing?"

"To Shirl," Lydia clarified.

Miguel turned and snapped his fingers. "Miguelito! Enrique!" The two boys jumped from the couch and ran over to him. Each took a bag and lugged it.

"They're too heavy," Lydia complained.

Miguel pointed the boys to the door. "Hurry, okay?" He gave Val a brief hug. "Thanks for letting us stay so long."

"That's what family's for," Val said, stiff in his arms.

"New Haven is not far," he said. "She'll be fine."

"She better be." Val's tone made it sound like a threat.

"I'm going to say good-bye to Shirl," Lydia said. "Want to come?"

He pretended to adjust the strap on the bag slung over his shoulder. "Say it for both of us."

IT WAS JUST for a little while, Lydia reminded herself as she made her way down the hall. Shirl was better off with Val for the time being. They'd come back for her once they'd gotten settled, once there was steady money coming in. Miguel made it all sound so sensible.

She pushed open the bedroom door, and a shaft of light from the hallway highlighted Shirl's sleeping face. Lydia sat on the edge of the bed and gazed on her daughter's features, soft as a ball of dough still taking shape.

They—Val, Miguel, and the teachers at Shirl's school—had all seen it long before Lydia and knew what it meant. Val and Miguel saw that Shirl wasn't as fast as her brothers had been at her age. Shirl's teachers noticed she didn't have the same motor skills as other seven year olds. Lydia refused to see, refused to know. There was a sense of unfairness to it all. She didn't think Shirl needed to be separated from other kids her age. She didn't like to see her daughter put on a special bus or placed into special education classes, but they—Val, Miguel, and the teachers at Shirl's school—said it was the best thing for Shirl, and it was for this and this alone that Lydia had to leave her.

"There are reasons," Lydia whispered to her daughter. "Good reasons, baby."

Sometimes it seemed to Lydia that Shirl was not slow at all. She was a fast learner; she picked up on things. When she was a baby, Shirl used to grab for Miguel. When she finally learned to walk, she followed him everywhere, but now she steered clear of her father. Lydia had never seen Miguel lift Shirl up or play with her the way he did with their boys. He kept his distance, blaming Lydia and the doctors for Shirl.

"It's just for a little while," Lydia whispered. She leaned over, kissed her sleeping child. "We'll get a real nice place. One where you can have your own room. We'll be back before you know it."

Lydia backed out and closed the bedroom door. Val waited in the hallway.

"I hate to leave her," Lydia said.

"She'll be fine," Val said. "You won't."

"We'll all be just fine," Lydia said. "I mean it. Don't meddle."

"I never meddle." Val pulled out a Marlboro. She struck the match and cupped her hand around the flame, bringing it up to the cigarette dangling from her lip. She did it carefully, as if she was out side in the middle of a strong wind and it was her last match. "You know how I feel about this. You shouldn't go so far away from your family."

"It's not that far," Lydia defended.

"I'm not talking about miles."

"Miguel's had to leave most of his family behind to come here. His sister is the only relative he's got in the States." Before she married Miguel, Lydia had never left Bedford-Stuyvesant.

"That's not the same." Val reached into her back pocket. The bills she pushed at Lydia were new and folded together so that there was no way of counting them. Lydia backed away from the money.

"What's it for?"

"Just a gift." Val grabbed her hand and slapped the money into it. "Just take it. It's enough for you to come back home."

Bail money, Lydia thought. Because Val didn't think she could make it on her own. She tried to hand the money back.

"Just in case." Val folded her arms across her chest, refusing to take it. The intercom buzzed long and loud, as if someone was lying on the button.

Lydia curled her fingers around the bills. "I'll call to check on her."

"Remember, that's for you and the boys." Val ushered her out. "Put it somewhere *he* won't see it."

So Lydia squeezed the money down her cleavage between her breasts, where Miguel had long since stopped looking.

"YOU'D THINK IT was another continent, not another state," Miguel said when she got into the car. He shrugged out of his coat and threw it across her lap. He wore his cotton button-down work shirt even though he hadn't worked for some time.

The boys couldn't be comfortable crunched into the backseat, hedged in by all of the bags. "They're tired," Lydia said. "We should have left in the morning."

"They're boys," Miguel said. "They're fine."

Lydia fingered the collar of his coat, fighting the urge to run back inside and get Shirl.

She didn't understand why they had to make the drive so late at night, and Miguel didn't bother to explain. Over in New Haven, Miguel's sister Lea was waiting up for them to make the drive from Bed-Stuy. Lydia had never met her and she feared to make a bad first impression. Lea ran a stationery store there and offered Miguel a job. For a little more than a year they had been spread out all over, doubled up in beds and sleeping on couches in Val's small two-bedroom apartment. Lydia could understand that Miguel didn't want to keep bumming off Val and that he wanted to be closer to his own people, but she still didn't see why they had to leave so late.

LEA ANSWERED THE bell on the first ring, opening the door, kissing the boys until they squirmed. She was nothing like Miguel, effusive where he was shy, white where he was brown. Her skin was the color of camellias and her eyebrows were penciled in reddish-brown half-moons of surprise. She was dressed for bed in a quilted robe and open-toed slippers. When she moved to gesture them in, Lydia first saw the candles.

"You still got them?" Miguel teased his sister as he brought the bags in.

"*Como no*," Lea said. "What would I do without them?"

"So many," he admonished.

"I get them from my store, so I give myself a discount. My candles," Lea said, waving a hand as if introducing them. "They're for Juan, my husband."

The candles were everywhere. Tall votive candles in cylindrical glasses, white outlines of saints on one side and long Spanish prayers on the other. All burning at once. Red, kelly green, purple, white, and deep blue. The candles were on the stereo's speakers. They surrounded the ceramic elephants on the end tables. Their heat made Lydia's head spin. Amidst the candles on the coffee table sat a statue of a woman. Miguel identified her as La Virgen de la Providencia, the Virgin of Providence, the patroness of Puerto Rico. She wore a white headdress and blue robes and held a baby Jesus in her arms. Lea fondled the statue lovingly. She said, "And when all else fails, I have her."

Lydia trembled, surrounded by the heat of so many fervent prayers and wishes. "Is your husband very sick?"

Lea laughed and smiled knowingly at her brother. "He has an affliction, yes. Of the heart. He strays. The candles are to keep him where he belongs."

ONCE LEA HAD gone to sleep and the boys had been put to bed, Miguel came to her. Lydia had their suitcases open, going through them in search of her nightgown.

He said, "You won't be alone. Spend time with Lea. She's your sister now."

He rubbed her shoulders and made plans. He said they could go to East Rock and look over the whole city. When it was warmer, he would take her and the kids to Lighthouse Beach. Lea would show them the university. "When the boys are older, they can go to Yale for college," he said. "If we can afford it."

Lydia thought of the money. "I need to change."

"There's time for that. Relax now." He touched her calf, gently squeezing.

"We can't," she said, jerking back. "The boys—"

"—are asleep," he said. "Take this off." He tugged at the hem of her blouse.

She wondered at the change in her husband. Miguel hadn't touched her in months. "Let me just go change in the bathroom?"

"It's nothing I haven't seen."

Lydia ran to the bathroom, flustered. With shaking hands, she tugged Val's money out of her cleavage and laid it on the sink counter.

The bills were crumpled now, slightly damp from being pressed near her skin. She had yet to count it. She was of a mind to show it to Miguel and tell him about Val's wild theories. Together, they would laugh at her sister's precaution. She would send the money back. She would *make* Val take it. Things would be different now. Lydia could feel the change in Miguel. He was happy now.

Lydia grabbed the wilted bills from the cool white counter and balled the money tight in her hand. Maybe she had better not tell Miguel just yet. She peeled off her coffee-colored knee-highs and stuffed the money into her nylon's left toe.

Miguel had pulled out the sofa bed and gotten in. The boys were asleep on opposite couches with blankets over them. Lydia placed her pile of clothing next to their bags, slid in beside Miguel and nudged him. "Honey?" He was fast asleep. Lydia turned on her side, but the candles wouldn't let her sleep. She worried that one would fall over, setting the house on fire while everyone slept. Two tall candles burned on the end table near Miguelito, and Lydia feared he would kick out in his sleep and knock them over. Gingerly, she moved her sister-in-law's candles over to another surface. She wanted to blow them out but did not wish to be rude.

One stubby blue candle burned on the end table near Enrique, and Lydia decided to move that one as well. As she reached to put the candle on the coffee table with the others, she bumped the Virgin of Providence and caught it before it fell, glad no one was awake to see her blunder. Holding the statue in her hands, she saw Shirl snuggled close to Val in bed, asleep with her mouth slightly parted, her middle and index fingers curled against each other near her cheek. Quickly, Lydia set the statue down. She gazed down at it, transfixed by the absorption between mother and child, unable to look away from the mother's inclined head and the child's answering gaze, filled with trust and wonder. Finally, she climbed into bed with Miguel and turned her back on the mother and child.

NO ONE IN the Fair Haven district ever passed Lea's store on Grand Avenue without going in. Men in guayaberas and hats came there to play their numbers. Women older than Lydia came to do their grocery shopping. Some came to hear Spanish spoken, to give their tongues a rest from English. With her combination brand of compassion and capitalism, Lea welcomed everyone but let no one loiter. "Everything is business," she told her customers. You could come and chat, but you had to pay for it. No one ever bought any stationery.

It took three weeks of Miguel working at Lea's store for her regulars to complain. Lea fired him and told him that Winchester Rifles, the factory where Juan worked, was hiring.

"I need a woman's touch," she said to Lydia. "You should come help me."

Although Lea advertised stationery, she mostly sold items for which people were homesick. Lydia was in charge of shelving and arranging the canned and boxed goods. Each day, she arranged cans of octopus, bags of tamarind candy, and tins of guava paste. Large cans of soda crackers and small bags of dried red beans. Jars and packets of spices: sofrito, sazon, and recaito. Twice a day, Lydia refilled the cooler with Maltas. Lea sold nothing fresh. Nothing that could go bad.

The younger women, it seemed, came mostly for the candles. Coming directly from mass at St. Francis on Ferry Street and from St. Rose on Blatchley, they showed up in Lea's store instead of going to Botanica Changó. They brought their problems, and Lea directed them to the shelves below the stationery where the prayer candles sat organized by height and color, the shorter and lighter candles to the left, the tallest and darkest to the right.

While selling these candles to the women, Lea told transformative stories, seducing listeners with tales of people who walked with a limp one day and could run and jump within a week after burning the candles. She told of a woman's husband who had left her more than twenty years ago. After burning the candles, he returned to beg her forgiveness. The work and the stories drove Lydia's days, kept her from missing Shirl more than was bearable, kept her from feeling that the problems which had plagued her and Miguel in Brooklyn had not disappeared but only gone into hiding. Miguel had moved them into their own apartment after two months of living with Lea, but—as before—Lydia hardly ever saw him, and he had yet to reach for her again. The stories made her feel a part of something and the work helped segment her loneliness into day and night. Listening to Lea's fantastic stories of fanatic relationships purchased for less than two dollars, the price of a prayer candle, and working among the enthralled listeners kept Lydia from calling Shirl too often and making a nuisance of herself, kept her out of the house while Miguel slept in preparation for the nights he spent using their car as a taxi, kept her from noticing that although Miguel had gone out many nights, he had not recently brought any money in.

IT WAS AMAZING how much damage the women could do. They sorted through the candles as if they were pricing diamonds. They reached behind and took the last ones in the back. They compared the length of the wicks and the opaqueness of the glass holders. Lydia had to spend hours organizing the candles in Lea's store, but she didn't mind. Sorting the candles, shelving, arranging and color-coding them gave her a sense of peace, a measure of sanity.

Lydia was dusting the candles when Josefina, a woman who bought her candles six at a time, came into the store. She was blowing hair out of her eyes as she walked, making a beeline for the back of the store where Lydia knelt with a tattered rag. "I want my money back!" Josefina demanded.

"What's wrong?" Lydia asked. Lea was in the back checking a shipment.

"This candle, it doesn't work," Josefina said, tears in her eyes.

Lea had confided that Josefina loved a man she couldn't have and—secretly—Lydia attributed the young woman's unluckiness in love to the ugly scar above her lip, guessing that it weakened her chances. She admired Josefina's persistence, a firm believer herself that holding on was sometimes best. "What's wrong with it?" she asked, her voice gentle with pity.

"I told you! It doesn't work!" Josefina shouted, the angry red scar above her lip stretching. "I want my money back!"

"Our store policy is no refunds. We can offer an exchange, or store credit."

"I come in here all the time!" Josefina cursed her low and quick in Spanish.

As one, the two women shouted for Lea.

Lea came running from the back room. "Que pasó?"

"This candle is a dud!" Josefina said, slamming it down in its brown paper bag. "I want my money back!"

Lea grabbed her chest as if it pained her.

"Don't tell me no refunds," Josefina said. She switched to Spanish and argued loudly and rapidly, pointing at Lydia and saying *negra*. Lea didn't argue back. She spoke soothingly and nodded. Placated, Josefina left with a bag of long-grain rice and six candles.

Later, after reshelving the candles, Lydia asked Lea if burning them had ever really worked. She wondered if they would help Shirl, if they would keep Miguel at home, if they would help her feel settled. She didn't have the heart to tell Miguel she didn't like it here.

"Do you believe in miracles?" Lea asked. Before Lydia could answer, she said, "They're a blessing and a curse and they don't just drop from the sky. The way my husband came to me, it was a miracle."

"How was it?" Lydia asked. She opened a box filled with jars of recaito and began to unpack them.

"Once, I went to Panamá, to Portabelo to visit the Cristo Negro. Do you know the legend? People come from all over the world to see him and get their wish. I didn't have anything to wish for until I became a woman in need of a husband. Did Miguel tell you we have two other sisters still back home in Ponce? I'm the oldest and both of my sisters got married before me. I tried everything, then I went to the Cristo Negro. He's in a small white church. There's nothing special on the outside, but inside there's a line. You light a candle and then you go and look in his eyes. There's a special spot where you stand. You say your prayer there and then you promise to give up something."

"Like Lent?"

"Something like that. You decide what to give up and how long, but it has to last a very long time. Maybe forever." Lea caught Lydia's look. "You don't believe me?"

Amidst all of the people there praying for loved ones to recover, praying for forgiveness for their sins, praying for children to be healthy and whole, Lea had asked for a husband. It seemed a narrow and selfish wish. "What did you give up?"

"I stood there on that spot almost five minutes until the people started to get mad. I looked into his eyes and wished for a husband and I waited. Then I felt it. His eyes were on me. He was looking back." Lea brought her hand down on the register and made the drawer clang open. "That was the sign. When I flew home I met Juan." Lea grinned, her eyebrows shooting all the way up to her forehead. "He was my Sky Cap. I came out with so many bags—I had bought a lot of relics—and he rushed over to me. He hailed me a taxi and carried my bags to the cab. I tried to pay him, but he wouldn't take my money. He put my bags in the trunk and then got in the cab and came home with me."

Lea's smile was triumphant and wide. "You see, it really works."

THAT FIRST TIME in Lea's kitchen, Lydia tried to light the white candle she'd taken from the store, but Lea rushed over and snuffed it out, angry. She scolded, "What are you thinking? Do you know how many people touched this before it came to you? All of their thoughts and wishes and prayers in here? You have to purify it first." Then she showed her how.

The second and third times were much easier. Lydia had five different candles burning for her in Lea's house in no time at all. She was grateful to Lea for allowing her to leave her candles there. She didn't want the boys asking questions. This way, she didn't have to watch the boys to make sure they didn't knock the candles over. Lea was a guardian; Lydia trusted her to make sure all the candles stayed lit.

LYDIA BEGAN TO dream of the candles at night, waking in a sweat, worried they'd been accidentally blown out. She dreamed that someone blew them out while she was watching and she was helpless to stop the culprit. She began to check on them over at Lea's several times a day, just to make sure. Once, during a routine check, she glimpsed that one of her wicks had burned down and Lea had not bothered to tell her. Appalled at Lea's carelessness, Lydia brought the candles into her home.

The red one came first. Lea said it would ward off unwanted presences. The blue one would give inner peace. The green one was to stop Miguel's wandering. There was even one guaranteed to make Shirl normal—healthy, fully cognizant, and whole—like all of the other children. Soon every free space was covered with a candle. Lydia kept a row of candles on her dresser, blocking out the attached mirror. She had candles on top of the kitchen counters. On top of the refrigerator. Next to the alarm clock. On top of the toilet's basin. On the windowsills and tables. Wherever she had room for one, Lydia put a candle there.

LYDIA WAS MAKING dinner, rolling pastelillos as Lea had taught her, when Miguelito and Enrique ran inside, begging for food.

"It's not done yet," she said. Enrique stared at a blue candle on the kitchen counter behind her bowl of dough. He reached out and traced the image of the virgin and child stamped on the glass with his fingertip. Lydia slapped his hand away.

"Ma, you like the candles better than us?" he asked, putting his fingers in his mouth to calm the sting.

Lydia watched the tiny flame flicker against the thick-coated glass. The candle was almost out; she would soon have to replace it. "Of course not," she said. "I love you two."

"Are we gonna open our own candle store like Titi Lea?" Enrique asked.

"Who told you that?"

"Miguelito," Enrique tattled.

"No, I didn't!" Miguelito said, punching his brother.

"Did too!"

"Did not!"

"Stop fighting!" Lydia said, separating them. "We're not opening a store."

"See, I told you," Enrique said and stuck his tongue out at Miguelito. Miguelito swiped at him.

"Stop that," Lydia said.

"So what do we have them for?" Enrique persisted.

Lydia didn't know how much to say. "Your aunt gave them to us. They help keep bad people away."

"Like the dentist," Miguelito whispered, teasing his brother.

"Like that lady that cut Papi!" Enrique shot back at him.

"What lady?" Lydia asked.

Enrique bit his lip. He looked at Miguelito. Miguelito shook his head at him. "Nothing," Enrique mumbled.

"It's too late for nothing," Lydia said. "Who cut your father? When was this? What lady?"

He shook his head.

"Do I know her?"

When Enrique still didn't answer, Lydia resorted to trickery. "She's not prettier than me, is she?"

"No way! She's ugly! Her hair is brown and her face is mean." He indicated her width with his hands. "She's real skinny, Ma. Not like you. And she's not brown like you either. She looks like Titi Lea and she has a real ugly mark on her lip."

Lydia reached for the counter to steady herself and overturned the bowl of flour. It turned on its side, spilling across the counter and knocking into the candle behind it. The tall cylinder of glass rocked on its base and teetered while the boys watched. Lydia couldn't stop it from falling. It fell on its side and rolled to the edge of the counter, where she caught it. She set it on its side, behind the bowl.

Josefina. Lea's friend. Lea, who had been like a sister. Lea, who had kept Lydia's candles. Lea, who had known.

"Ma, you mad at me?" Enrique asked.

"No," Lydia said flatly. There was only one way for them to know. They had obviously cut school. She would deal with that later. "Was Josefina in here?"

"Papi was dragging her down the stairs and his arm was bleeding. He was yelling at her for cutting him and she was trying to put her shoes on. And then Miguelito said he wanted to go and punch her in the face, but I didn't let him even when he pushed me down," Enrique said.

Lydia listened without saying a word.

Enrique asked, "Ma, was I right to stop Miguelito?"

Miguelito argued, "Ma, I wasn't really gonna punch her."

Lydia gave them money and sent them out to play.

MIGUEL TOLD HER he had been in a fight.

Lydia opened the silverware drawer and ran her fingers over the knives, wondering which one Josefina had used. She closed the drawer and saw Josefina in the kitchen, moving through the house like she owned it. She wondered if Josefina had eaten their food, sat on their couch, looked through their records, made herself comfortable.

She had, of course, been in their bed.

Somewhere within her breast Lydia had kept a wish steadily burning, like a candle, and now its thin flame flickered, sputtering with what she now knew.

Walking slowly through the apartment, Lydia looked with all-seeing eyes. Her possessions no longer seemed hers. Now they looked as if they belonged to someone else. And they had. She and Miguel had furnished the apartment with thrift-store furniture that had been laughed on, hated on, and worn out by people she would never meet. She forced herself to walk to the bedroom. They'd bought the bedroom set intact from the thrift store and it had been like brand new. The store manager told her the couple who owned it had split up suddenly and gone their separate ways. Since neither one had wanted the other to have the set, they'd decided to sell it. Lydia hadn't believed the manager. She'd chalked it up as a yarn spun to get her money, but now she thought about the couple and wondered what had made their plans go awry. For surely, like her, they had planned to stick it out, had wished for things to work.

Lydia returned to the kitchen. She cleaned up the spilled flour, wiping down the counter with a wet dishrag. Behind the bowl lay the candle that had fallen. Lydia grasped the thick glass cylinder, blackened from the smothered flame, still warm to her touch, and set it upright once more. She didn't bother to light it.

The Luckiest Man in the World

THE TITIS ARE in the kitchen fighting over the arroz con pollo. They are twins—Alma y Lara—and they fight over everything, like who's the youngest (Lara says it's her by ten minutes) and whose food tastes better. They are making everyone wait to eat. When we get there—me; my twin, Cheo; my younger brother, Luis; and my father—my aunts' boyfriends are smoking at the table, forlorn, like two poor putos as my aunts try to make them say whose arroz con pollo is best. The titis beckon us into the kitchen. Yali warns us with her eyes not to get embroiled in the battle. But we are hungry and we don't care.

"Which is better?" Titi Alma asks, coming at me and Cheo with spoons heaping with rice, olives, and chicken.

We frown hard, giving what we hope are discerning looks. We tell her that we can't know after just one bite.

"Which do you prefer?" Titi Lara asks, covering Luis's eyes with one hand and pushing a spoon toward his mouth with the other.

"I need to taste it again," he says.

We are smarter than the average ten year olds; we vacillate, we refuse to confirm until we have eaten our fill. Titi Lara catches on and drives us out of the kitchen, chasing after us with a wooden spoon. "Go play outside," she says.

This is fine with us.

"¡Ven acá, Yali!" I yell.

"She can't go," Titi Alma says over her shoulder.

"You know she hurt herself," Titi Lara reminds us.

I had forgotten Yali's broken fingers and how I was responsible for them. I'd been trying to teach her a trick on the swings the last time we were here. I'd pushed her too hard and she came down too fast, getting three of her fingers caught in the metal chain links right at the moment when she should have done a 360 on the swing and jumped over the fence like I showed her.

I look at my brothers. Then I look at Yali. Her brown face with the baby hair brushed back from her forehead and secured by a headband, her thick eyebrows and the small dark hairs that crept along her upper lip made her beautiful to me. Thanks to me she had lost her two front teeth in the second grade, and her new adult teeth had not grown in until last summer. I love the new toothy smile she smiles at me when she shows me her broken fingers and says, "Go ahead, Coquito. No me importa."

"I'll keep her company," I say, nudging my brothers away. "You go without me."

"You don't want to keep her company," Cheo whispers. "You just want to suck her tetas."

"And she doesn't even have any yet," Luis says.

"Cállate, pendejos," I say, pushing them away.

"Ten cuidado puto," Cheo says seriously. He will not condescend to remind me that he is older by four hours. My whole family treats those four hours as though they are four years. In their eyes, I am a lesser version of my brother. Cheo was greedy in the womb and I got all the leftovers. So I am small and scrawny, with a widespread face and eyes like a frog. And my family is not kind. They never call me by my real name, Cristofer. Instead, they call me Coquito after that little frog that only lives in El Yunque, the rainforest in Puerto Rico.

WE, YALI AND I, go to her bedroom to play until we can eat.

"Does it hurt?" I ask stupidly, looking at the three broken fingers wrapped in gauze and banded in thick white tape. She looks at me. She is too kind to call me tonto, the idiot that I am.

"I can't jump rope," she says. "I can't even braid my own hair."

"Who did that, then?" I ask, pointing stupidly to her braided hair.

"Constanza did it for me at lunchtime today. See?" she says, turning her back to me.

That braid of hers is a treacherous thing. Long and black, braided loose and flimsy, shining dark. A small red rubber band contained all of it except for a little tail that curled under at the bottom. I had only touched Yali's hair once in my life, to cut a chunk of it off as a prank and a sign of my love for her. The titis had to cut three inches off Yali's hair to even out the damage I had done. That was two years ago. I touch it now and feel like it belongs to me.

Minutes pass in which I say nothing to her. It is as much a surprise to me when I hear my thoughts given sound. "Let's play doctor," I say.

Yali looks at me warily. I had played too many pranks on her to be angry at her skepticism. She had a right. "En serio," I say and cross my heart.

"Okay," she says.

"Doctora, I don't feel well," I say.

"Where does it hurt?" she asks.

"Everywhere," I groan. "Especially here." I take her good hand and put it on me.

Yali's eyes widen, her thick bushy eyebrows shoot straight up her forehead. A fear in her eyes makes me hold on to her.

Yali pulls away, taking her hand with her.

I put it back again. "What if someone comes?" she asks, shaking her head, that braid of hers flicking over her shoulder.

I am sure that no one will because the adults have been playing bachata and salsa in the living room for some time now. Tito Nieves, Juan Luis Guerra, La India. "Preciosa" is playing now. My father always played it to make the titis cry. Hearing "Preciosa" tells me that they have forgotten about us.

"Está bien, Yali," I say, pressing her hand to keep it there.

"It's weird." She squirms.

"Wait," I say, "don't take your hand away."

"Why not?"

"It's making me feel better."

She looks at me with her head tilted to the side, like maybe she is seeing through me.

"Medicina," I say.

";Seguro?"

"Si," I say. "Claro."

"LET ME SEE IT," Yali says after a few moments of rubbing back and forth across my zipper.

"You let me see first."

"No," she says, resolute, reaching for my zipper.

"Then you have to let me feel."

I pull her by the hem of her dress, by the scalloped laces sewed onto denim, until she is on top of me. It's awkward, her knees bump my thighs, but I play it cool so she won't know that now that I've got her here I don't know what to do with her.

"Nadie Como Ella" is playing in the sala. I move under her, trying to catch the strain of it, holding her to make her copy my movements. I have one hand on her hip, the other is touching the tail of her black braid. The titis are in the kitchen still arguing over the two identical dishes. By now my father is drunk and asleep on the couch, the boyfriends are playing dominoes and smoking at the kitchen table, my brothers are outside playing on the stoop ignoring the girls jumping rope in front of them to get their attention and grabbing at the girls who walk by and pretend to ignore them. I can look into Yali's wide-open eyes and see all of them with this newly acquired vision. What I see does not impress me. None of them are where I am, none have what I have, none can feel what I am feeling at this moment. I have it. Suerte. Luck. I am a man now, a lucky man, even though I'm only ten. None of them are as lucky as me. I am not asleep; I am not drunk; no one is keeping me waiting or making me play stupid games. I am right here.

"Close your eyes," Yali says.

"Why?"

"So I can see you."

But I could not close my eyes. She could disappear any minute and I'd be on the stoop with Cheo and Luis. And I want to be right here with Yali's thick eyebrows, her brown face, the tiny hard buds of her breasts straining under her blouse, her two legs cupping my hips and pressing the thin panel of her cotton panties against me, her small hand on my shoulder, the wide eyes looking down at me warm and trusting and curious as she bites her lip to keep quiet, and that black braid entangling my hand, the silk of it rubbing my palm and five fingers. That braid makes everything real. I grab it—lightly—just to make sure.

Remembering

THE FIRST PLACE Julio went, instead of coming home to us, was to his boy Jim's house. A week passed before we even knew he was back. Old Cleo hit the number and asked me to tell my brother to drop by and see him so he could hit him off now that he was back. Julio had been gone for almost three months, but Cleo had been owing him the money for more than a year.

I tell Pops that Julio is back in town.

"Go and get him," Pops says. "Go and bring your brother home."

I tell him that he is at Jim's. Pops wants Julio to come home but he doesn't want him to know that he's concerned.

"He belongs here with us," Pops says. "But don't tell him I said it."

JULIO HAD BEEN hinting for some time about moving out on his own once he turned eighteen. But we never thought he would do it. He had to wait until then to be legally free of Pops first. 'Cause when Julio first talked about leaving, Pops had not even stirred out of his chair in front of the living room TV to say in Spanish, "Do it and I'll drag you back here and beat your ass. You're my son and my responsibility. You run out there causing trouble, and these fucking cops will bring it right to my face. I ain't going to jail for you, pato. I'll knock your head in first."

And we knew he would too. Pops didn't like to be bothered. When either of us cut up in school and the administrators called home to rat us out, Pops would yell at them for bothering him and disturbing his peace. And then he'd kick our asses.

Pops was a big man. A red-faced Puerto Rican with a halo of nappy hair and a ruddy, pock-marked face. He'd done a little amateur boxing in his day, and he still carried the weight with him although it was melting into fat now. Pops was a mean bastard too. He'd left Puerto Rico for the United States not because he'd wanted to, but because he'd gotten into trouble and had no other choice.

He and Julio liked to go at it with each other. Their fights had gotten worse the closer Julio got to turning eighteen. Two weeks before his birthday, they were fighting every day. The night before his birthday, they exploded on each other. The next morning Julio was gone.

I COULD SAY that I missed him. Sometimes it was like we were all we had, what with a crazy father and a mother in Philadelphia that I couldn't remember. Pops could always push Julio's buttons whenever he brought up our mom. Julio knew her longer than me, and he never liked it when Pops criticized the way she raised us. Pops said she had been raising us to be Americans and that she had made us soft. Julio was sensitive when it came to our mother because he still remembered her. I never could remember things.

I don't remember the night that Pops came for us, but I heard the story enough for it to feel like my own memory. We were living in Philadelphia. To hear Pops tell the story, he had driven over from New York on one of his frequent trips to check on us and bring her some money for us. To hear Julio tell it, Pops only came like once or twice in our whole lives. Julio'd had a birthday and turned eight a month before (Pops had not shown up for that). So when Pops got there, he'd asked my brother his age. He'd asked him in Spanish and Julio hadn't understood him. Pops got so pissed that we were forgetting our Spanish that he took us back to Brooklyn that night with nothing but the clothes on our backs.

He said he took us back with him to make us harder, to make us men. He taught us the few things he knew. He taught us how to box. Pops used to practice on us. If we weren't quick enough, we'd catch it. We sometimes went to school with black eyes and our teachers left us alone because they all thought it was best to just let us kill each other.

"NO, NOT LIKE THAT," Pops would say, putting his meaty hand over one of ours to reposition the alignment of our fingers for the fist.

"A jab is quicker than that. Like *pow* in the eye before the next man even sees you coming. Try it again. Otra vez. Oye, not like that. Mira, like this. Again. Una mas. Otra vez. Jab. Right. Hook. Uppercut. Finish it off. Mira, this is a combination. What the hell are you doing, hijo? Otra vez."

He would make us spar with each other for practice, even though Julio was always bigger than me and could put more of his weight behind a blow. Even though it was never a fair fight.

Pops would say, "It's a cruel world, muchacho. Don't let nobody tell you different. If somebody hit you, hit them back. And you get the next guy before he can get you. And once you get him, you make sure he don't get up or he'll get you back."

Little wonder we never asked him what made him have to leave PR in such a hurry.

I TELL MY pops that Julio probably don't want to be found, but he sends me out to Jim's anyway. To try.

I remember Jim. A string bean. Slim Jim, we called him. Slight and awkward, as if he'd recently had a growth spurt and wasn't yet used to being in his new, taller body. Julio always locked me out of his room when Jim came over. They would closet themselves in that room for what seemed like hours, smoking weed and talking shit. They'd have the boom box turned all the way up, blaring Run-DMC, Kurtis Blow, and Grandmaster Flash so I couldn't hear. The smell of marijuana would seep out from under the door where they'd tried to stop the space up with a towel. Sometimes I knelt down by the door and whiffed, praying for a contact high.

When I get to Jim's building and ring the bell, the intercom comes on like the garbled speech at a drive-in's talk box. Who is it? sounds like *whizzit*.

"It's me. It's Manny," I answer, knowing he can't make out what I'm saying.

No one buzzes me in. I wait. Two minutes go by. Then three, four, and five. Young boys on the corner eye me warily, trying to figure out if I'm 5-0 or just a punk. They are eighteen, nineteen maybe, with faces still smooth and fledgling mustaches and goatees that look more like dark patches of rough skin than hair. Big men on the corner, pagers on their belts, cell phones in the pockets of oversized denim jackets.

In front of the Van Dyke projects on Mother Gaston and Junius where Jim lives, the playground looks like a prehistoric garden. Stone turtles, dolphins, and whales meant for climbing support the weight of the girls who are sitting on them, smoking. The girls are young, but they don't look it under the layers of makeup that disguise their faces. Their bodies are grown and they won't let you forget that. They wear the type of clothing that forces you to see them only in parts—as breasts and abdomens and hips and thighs. I can tell which of them have already had babies. I can tell which of them will let me screw them behind the dumpster for twenty bucks.

A man runs up the steps to the building and keys in his code, entering and swinging the door behind him. I catch the door. I am inside now, and what I see is the same inside every project in Brooklyn. Walls painted bright orange or dark green. Two elevators, only one of which works. Waiting for the other one is a joke. It will come down and thirty people will try to crowd in at once like they're on the subway. Dank stairways that smell of piss, graffiti leading the way up every flight of stairs: *Raheem loves Babee* sprayed in a heart with the year on the bottom.

Jim yells out from his side of the door. "Who is it?"

"Manny," I say.

"Who?"

"Manuel."

I hear the slide of the peephole being uncovered. Jim opens the door but doesn't give me a pound and doesn't let me in.

"What you want?"

"Is my brother here?"

Jim is as skinny as ever. An oversized football jersey hangs off his bony shoulders. He looks back over his shoulder at someone or something. Then he shakes his head.

"Nah, I ain't seen your brother."

"You must think I'm stupid," I say.

He shrugs.

"Maybe."

I TELL POPS the search is a no-go, but he's not going to hear that. He takes it as an insult that Julio would come back and not come to see us, even just to visit.

"It's like he's spitting in my face," Pops says. "You bring him back, Manny."

"What if he don't want to come?"

"Make him."

I KEEP TRYING. I choose different times of the day, hoping to catch him unawares. I come by when I think Jim is at work and Julio will have to answer the door. I come by when I think it's time for the mail to be delivered. I come by when I think it's time for them to go food shopping. I thought I saw him once as I was turning the corner to get to Van Dyke. A young man with Julio's body, Julio's build. I called his name, but the man picked up speed and ran back the way he'd come.

"Let's try this again," I say to Jim. "Is Julio here?"

Jim doesn't answer. The TV is blaring behind the door. I hear the awkward dubbed-over voices of a bad Kung-Fu movie.

"Can I come in and talk to my brother?"

"Can't let you do that."

"This is bullshit," I say. "Why don't you just let me in?"

"Nah, you can't come in here."

"Maybe you better tell him I'm here," I say. Jim turns away from the door, holding it tightly with his hands so I can't push my way through. He is speaking to someone.

"Tell him Pops said he better come back home."

"Maybe he doesn't want to see him," Jim says.

"Well he's going to see me one way or another. If it's not now, I'll just keep coming back. I know where to find him. Tell him that," I say.

Jim turns again, whispering to my brother who is evidently standing behind him just out of my line of vision.

"Tell him I said it's time for him to come home," I say.

Jim turns back to me.

"He says he's not here."

THE THING WITH Julio and Pops is difficult and different than any other shit I ever seen. My brother is a junior, and I guess that's supposed to mean something. Pops has always been harder on him than me. But the result is the same. Me and Julio both hate his ass. If I had the money, I'd move out too, but I ain't got nowhere to go.

So if I wanna keep a roof over my head, Pops makes it clear that I got to do this job and bring my brother back. But we all already know what's gonna happen if he does come back. They'll be fighting each other like crazy again. It's terrible the way they go at each other. Pops will be in his room watching Spanish porn and drinking rum. My brother will be in his room listening to music and getting high. Then they'll both come out of their rooms at the same time. On their way to take a piss or to get something from the kitchen or whatever. They'll be in each other's way. And that's how easy it will start. Over some "You move out of my way," and some "No. I was here first" shit. Pops wants Julio to move first out of respect for his position and age. Julio won't because he says Pops ain't never done nothing to earn his respect. Then Pops goes on about how Julio is ungrateful. The liquor makes his tongue run to the topic of our mother, and Pops will blame his behavior on the way our mother raised him. And that will be it. The voices get louder, and even the bass from my stereo can't cover up their fighting as they shout and cuss and start to whale on each other, fighting as each one protects his square of space and blocks the other from advancing. I watched it once after I tried to pull them apart and got my lip busted for the trouble. They were both solid men, squat like. It was like watching two evenly matched rams butting heads.

Our father was a good three hundred pounds. He was a fighter. He'd show us pictures back from his boxing days. We didn't ever want to see pictures of what happened to the other guy. Pops had a penchant for fighting, a refusal to conform and do things the way they were written, the way other people wanted them done. That was our father. It got him beat up a lot, but the tenacity was something you had to admire from a distance. He was the little guy that kept going head up against the system, knocking his roach-hard skull against the brick wall, like that poem they made us read when we graduated from the eighth grade about our heads being bloodied but unbowed. He would just keep going at it, pushing through instead of going around, whaling away at the obstacles in front of him. The only thing was that sometimes we were the obstacles. And we got whaled on too.

MY NEXT TRIP pays off.

Jim opens the door, clearly not surprised to see me.

"He's not here," he says.

"Look, we've tried that one before. I'm getting tired of this. I want to see him. Why can't I just see him?"

"That's between the two of you," he says. "He don't want to go home, I can't make him. I'm sure you know the deal."

"What, you his spokesperson now?"

"Yo, I don't have time for some ill shit like this."

"I just want to see him and I'm gonna keep coming here until I can. And if that doesn't work, I'll wait around corners and loaf in the pizza shop or the Associated or anywhere that I know he might go. You're gonna get pretty tired of seeing my face."

"I'm already tired," Jim says. "Y'all act like a bunch of kids."

"I got a message for him."

"Write a letter," he says, edging the door toward my face.

"I'm serious!" I say, blocking the door with my arm.

And then I am. I'm here now not just to keep my father happy, not just to run an errand, but to see my brother. The months without him were rough. It was like our place was empty. Me and Pops ain't have much to say to each other without Julio there. And I wanted to know where he had gone and what had made him come back. I had been scared the first couple of days until I realized that if something bad happened, I would be able to feel it. I wanted to know if he hated me too now, just like Pops, even though I hadn't ever done anything to him. I wondered if I was guilty by association. And I am thinking of those days when we used to be close before he grew up and sat holed up in his room watching music videos, smoking weed, leaving me behind. Julio used to tell me stories about our mother, since I was too young to remember on my own. The night we left Philadelphia, we sat in the back of Pops' beat-up car and I cried like I would never stop. Julio pinched me and told me to stop crying. Julio told me this, so I don't know if it's true, but he said that Mami kissed us when she put us to bed every night. And that she smelled like lemons and pears. And that she had just bought him a red and black dirt bike for his birthday that Pops wouldn't let him bring to New York. In the car that night he whispered these things about her so I wouldn't forget them. He was smarter than I was and he knew we would never see her again. So he stopped my tears with memories. To this day, I don't remember much of anything about her, but if she was the kind of mother who would buy her kid a bike, then I know I must have loved her.

I use the last weapon I have. I tell Jim, maybe Julio's too scared to see me.

Jim turns to look behind him, but he doesn't speak to anyone. He just stands there for a moment, looking over his shoulder. Then he turns back to me.

"Come back tomorrow," Jim says.

THE NEXT DAY, at two, Julio opens the door. I can't tell if he is surprised or not.

"I thought you were Jim," he says.

I'm not.

Julio is dressed like something out of a Rocky movie; he looks like a boxer training for his big break. His hooded sweatshirt is too tight and the black letters of our high school emblazoned on it are chipped and peeling away. He wears shorts over sweat pants and jogs in place in front of me.

"Can I come in?"

"I guess. I don't care."

He lets me in and closes the door behind me. I try to give him dap, but his hands are icy.

We are sitting down on the edge of Jim's couch like it's only natural. I can feel Julio's tension pointing at me. I wonder how long I have before he throws me out. He's trying to act cool, but he's still my brother and I know him better than that.

Jim's house is nothing like Pop's. This living room is almost empty: just this couch, a standing lamp and an old stereo system with a record player on the top level instead of a CD player. No coffee table, no rug, no nothing that would make it look comfortable. A Spartan's lair. Julio must love it. When we were kids, my room was wallpapered with posters of Lisa Lisa, Sheila E., and Vanity, littered with Transformers and Star Wars figures and X-Men comics, and Julio's room resembled a prison. He had a bed, a desk, a chair, a lamp, and a small radio he'd bought on his thirteenth birthday.

"You like?" he asks. "Nice, huh?"

"I knew you would think so," I say.

Out of nowhere, he smiles at me. I can't help smiling back. I always hated his room. But at least it's a start. He's not exactly welcoming me with open arms, but he hasn't kicked me out either. I ease back onto the couch, feeling the coils coming through the material and scratching the backs of my thighs.

I figure we may as well get this over with. Julio knows why I am here. So I just say it.

"Pops wants you to come back."

"I can't do that. You know that. He send you here just to tell me that?"

"He said you're spitting in his face. You know he'd be looking for you."

"Tell him to kiss my culo," Julio says. "He can't touch me anymore. I'm free."

"Where did you go?"

"I had been thinking a lot about some things. About when we were little. Do you remember?"

"Yeah," I say. "We were young. I was younger."

"Don't be smart. Oye. Pops never acted like he gave a shit if we lived or died, but it was so important for him to keep us away from Mami. You ever wonder what the deal was between them?"

"Yeah, sometimes," I say, lying. The truth was that I knew better than to wonder about things like that because they would eat me up. I don't wonder about a lot of things. I'm fast on my way to becoming mediocre.

"Yeah. Well. I could never figure it out. Pops didn't want us to grow up black."

"What are you talking about?" I asked as my stomach started to tighten on itself. It sounded to me like I was going to hear nasty things about my father. And I wasn't ready for them. I still had three years to go before I could move out. I didn't want to hear it if what Julio was going to tell me would make me want to leave.

I said, "Never mind, don't tell me."

"No, you gotta hear this."

"I don't want to hear it."

"Why, is he some type of fucking saint now that I'm gone that you can't listen to the truth," he shouted.

I jumped up from the couch.

"Leave it!"

Julio grabbed me by my arm. "Listen, you're the one that kept coming here after me. I didn't want to have to tell you until I found a good way to say it."

I put my hands over my ears like I was back in grade school. But Julio's words made it through anyway.

He said, "You know what it was like when he first came over here? When Pops came over here, he thought everybody was the same.

Black. Puerto-Rican. It was all the same to him. Until he got with Mami and people started to treat him differently. Like he was black. And it wasn't the same at all. He could look as black as he wanted to, but as long as he spoke that Spanish and had that funny accent, nobody said nothing. They gave him jobs. They treated him good. Not as good as a blanco, but not as bad as a black. That's when he started to be different. He wasn't always like he was with us. Don't you understand what he did to us?"

Julio wanted me to understand something I couldn't let myself understand.

"He didn't want us to be black," Julio said.

"Stop it," I said.

"He didn't want to have to feel ashamed of us," he said.

"Shut up!" I said, trying to pull away.

Julio gets up in my face so there is nowhere to go. He squeezes my arm.

"He didn't want to look down on us and think he was better than us, the way he felt with Mami!"

"Don't talk about my father like that," I shout. It's one thing to hate him in silence. It's another thing to say it out loud. I lash out and deck Julio without thinking, my fist connecting with his hard jaw. I don't want to think of the man Pops was before we came along or all that it must have taken to change him and crush him into the father we ended up with.

"Coño, what the fuck is wrong with you? You act just like Pops. Yeah, you're his son all right."

Julio shakes off the blow, checking his mouth for blood. He pushes me across the room, "Yeah, he's your father. That's for sure. Only yours, you son of a—"

I'm on him in an instant. Fighting is easy for us. It's second nature, the only gift our father has ever given to us. Kicking ass is something I can do with my eyes closed. But Julio is bigger than me. And stronger. And meaner. But I am savage. I don't give up. I fight against all that I have learned.

I lower my shoulder and throw it into his chest, knocking the wind out of him. We crash to the floor, grappling and landing blows wherever and whenever we can. And I'm not scared anymore of saying or doing the wrong thing. I just feel this connection with my brother, however primal, and it's telling me that I'm not a stranger to him anymore.

I fight for breath. My lungs burn.

"Pops was really missing you," I say. "He's not like he used to be. He wanted me to tell you to come back, but he didn't want me to let you know he said it. He wants you think he don't care, but it's not true," I say.

In his own way, Pops loved us. It was something I couldn't see until Julio ran away. The tough, hard demeanor our father had put up as a front crumbled once Julio was gone. He didn't blame himself for making Julio run, he was not that enlightened, but he felt the absence and the loss. There was no one there to yell at because I tried my hardest to stay out of his way. I still had three more years to go before I could leave without worrying about Pops dragging my ass back. And I wasn't enough of a challenge for him anyway. Julio was more like him, so fighting with him was tougher, like fighting your own shadow. After Julio first left, Pops would stay up all night in his chair in the living room, facing the door, waiting for Julio to come back. When the days turned to weeks and months, he moved to the bed. But he was still waiting. He'd lie in the bed with his door open and the TV turned down low so that he could be the first one to hear Julio unlock the door with his key. He said he was waiting to kick Julio's ass, but I knew better.

Julio nods. He won't argue and he won't agree. He gets in a lucky punch to my left eye, and I try to block my face and kick his feet out from underneath him at the same time.

I deliver a powerful right and knock him flat on his back and pin him there. We are winded. But I have won the right, so I ask him.

"Where did you go?"

He looks as if he will not answer me, even though my elbow is in his throat.

"Philadelphia," he whispers, as if the walls have ears.

"I found her," he says.

His words make me release him. I back away and sit on the floor like a little kid. Pops and I thought maybe he'd done something crazy like joined the army or the Job Corps or something like that. But not something as crazy as this. I never guessed that he would go looking for our mother.

"How?"

"She wasn't lost."

"I didn't remember her," he says. "Until she opened the door. She was still there. In the same place. All this time."

"She still had our pictures on the coffee tables. And the frames were clean. I think she dusted them every day," he said.

It wasn't far. A train ride to the Port Authority. Hopping onto the New Jersey Transit. A switch to SEPTA. It could be done in under three hours for less than thirty bucks. But thirty bucks may as well have been a million, and Philadelphia may as well have been as far away as the moon and the stars for us and how we were raised. I couldn't believe Julio had done it.

He says, "I didn't go right away. I hung around here, sold a little to get up some cream so I could go. Then I still waited. I didn't know what I was going to say. I mean, how do you introduce yourself? I didn't know what to say to my own mother."

"What did you say?"

"I must have chilled in Philly a good month before I actually rang the bell and stayed long enough for her to answer it. The first couple of times I would ring the bell and then jet. But one time I made myself stay. She opened the door and saw me. And then I didn't have to say anything at all. She knew me," he said.

She remembered.

I shake my head. There is nothing I can say. Julio has more balls than me. I would have convinced myself to turn back before I tried. I would have thought of all the reasons to stay behind and leave things the way they were. Memories could make you vulnerable. There was pain in remembering. You could never go back to the things that you remembered. And if you could, it wouldn't be the same. And as long as you remembered, you could never move forward. You were stuck in the middle. Trapped.

But she had remembered.

In that moment, I see my brother at the door. Ringing the bell. Being taken in. Being made to feel as if he had never left. Remembering and being remembered.

I wish I had gone, too. I wish I had seen her. I wish I could remember the breadth of her smile, the touch of her fingertips, anything. Anything at all.

"Did she say anything?" I ask.

"When I opened the door, she said, 'You didn't forget me.'"

"I told her I never did," Julio says.

I say, "Did she ask for me?"

Julio makes a face at me.

"She asked for you, tonto. Como no."

I HAD ONE memory, one thing that I could remember on my own without coaxing and repetition.

Our mother made us get our hair cut every Saturday so we would look presentable for church on Sunday. One Saturday, the barber had pressed too hard with the clippers while shaping my front, and the sharp metal teeth had pressed into my forehead while he was etching a side part into my scalp. It would have just been a small cut that would have healed in a day or two had I not jumped and made it worse. The cut was small but deep and my skin was prone to scar. A keloid took the place of the cut once it healed and all I have to remember from the days with her was an almost imperceptible patch of scarred tissue on my forehead that I could probe the length of with my index finger.

And now I remember too. I say what Julio has told me about our mother, what has now become my memory. I used to say it over and over again before going to bed at night. "Don't forget me," is what Julio said she said when she watched our father drag us away. But I couldn't forget what I never remembered. I closed my eyes and said our memories.

"Mami's face is brown and her hair is black. She used to make us pies. She liked to cook pancakes for breakfast on Sunday. She always made us go to church. But we had to shine our shoes first. She pulled our ears when we spoke out of turn. But she kissed us good-night. Every night."

"Every night," Julio said.

It's funny, the things you forget. Until someone reminds you. If Pops had it his way, he'd have us thinking we were born without a mother, like that myth of the Greek goddess who popped out of somebody's head. He never spoke of her unless he was goading Julio. He never even mentioned her name. We had no pictures of her. Pops figured we were better off without her. In his eyes, she was black and Americano and could not have been trusted to raise us on her own. Once, he had said that if he had left it up to her we would have learned to forget Spanish and we would have grown up thinking we were black. We would not have known who we were. He had done such a good job of making me forget her that if I had walked past her on the street I would not have recognized my own mother.

But Julio refused to forget. Maybe it was because he was older. Or just because he was stubborn, but Pops could never make him do the things he wanted.

It's amazing the things you could remember if you wanted to. Julio couldn't remember to add the accent marks on his words when he wrote in Spanish. He couldn't remember to dump the trash down the incinerator after Pops had told him like five times. Or to come home at a decent hour or to brush his teeth, he could go for days at a time without doing that. But he could remember the first address he had ever memorized, the street number to a home he couldn't recall; he could summon up our mother's address and apartment number from where the memories of them had lain buried for ten years. He could remember it clearly enough to go straight there as if he'd never left.

"Did she remember us?" I ask.

Julio looks offended, but he must not be because he doesn't swipe at me. "Of course," he says.

"What did she do?"

"She cried," he said. "She cried a whole lot."

Then we sit there. I try to conjure her face, to see her face distorted with crying, her eyes red with tears and her cheeks swollen and puffy, but behind my eyes there is no image. Only darkness.

That's when we hear the lock turning and know that Jim is back. We lunge for each other and jump right back into the fighting, losing no time as we pretend to kill each other. We don't want to get caught looking sappy. Jim comes in with his arms full of groceries. He drops them right in front of the door and quickly pulls us apart.

"Yo, break it up! Now!" he yells, when Julio tries to duck around him and lunge for me.

Jim is disgusted with both of us.

"I told you," he says. "A bunch of babies is just what I said and I was right. Y'all need to grow up and stop acting like this. When are y'all gonna learn anything?"

Neither of us can catch our breath enough to make a satisfactory answer to him. We nod apologies, breathing harshly, wiping our noses, checking for blood, grinning from ear to ear.

Jim takes the groceries into the kitchen. Once he leaves the room, Julio shoves me lightly and smiles crookedly. I shove him back, feeling freer and better than I have felt in years. I start to tell him so, but he cuts me off.

"I can still beat you," he says.

The Last Hurricane

HURRICANES THAT HIT Puerto Rico have Americano names like Alice, and even when they name one Hugo the weathermen don't pronounce it correctly. Hurricanes never have the names of your children or relatives. Names like Milagros or Rafael.

When they find out that another hurricane is coming your way, your relatives on the mainland—in New Haven, Hartford, Philadelphia, Newark, and New York—always call and ask if you are ready. If you need anything. They want to send you and the children things to help you cope.

But you know the truth.

They want to send you and the children things to ease the guilt that they feel as they sit in their safe condos and co-ops with central air and all the other amenities, as they put their feet up to watch the news for the weather report, smug that they are safe and warm while you are . . . not.

"What will you need?" they ask.

Clean water.

Hot water.

Ice.

Electricity.

None of which they can provide.

They want to send blankets, powdered milk, deodorant, diapers. "This is not St. Croix," you say. Besides, your children are too old for diapers. Your relatives have watched one too many news reports.

The winds of the last hurricane that hit your town knocked out all the power lines for days, and you had no light, no heat, no phone. It really wasn't that bad because you live in Carolina, near enough to San Juan and the turistas so that the problem was fixed pronto. But you heard that the people who lived farther out where the turistas hardly ever went had it real bad—no power for almost three weeks.

Imagine if you lived there.

THE LAST HURRICANE knocked over the two coconut trees in front of your house and wiped out the crab and chicken pens in the back-yard. You heard the chickens squawk as the winds carried them away as you sat in the dark with the wind howling in your ears and your hijo Rafael crying because it was his job to bring the chickens in and he forgot. You tried to shush him by reminding him that he was your jibarito, but Milagros was louder than you as she called him tonto and slapped at whatever parts of him she could find in the dark.

During the time of a hurricane, it is not good to be alone. Which is why you are glad you still have the hijos. Although it is dark and you cannot see their two faces, you cross from one end of the room to the other after you have sent them to bed, sitting by their sides and placing your palms on their foreheads. Your hijos smell sweet in the darkness; the scent of the tembleque they had for dessert lingers in their partly opened mouths. On a night like this, you don't bother them about brushing their teeth before bed.

"Está bien," you say.

"Calmase."

"Estoy aquí."

You trace their worried cheeks. You pinch their noses for fun, to cheer them up, glad that you cannot see their eyes in the dark. You will sleep lightly tonight because your children cry in their sleep whenever the winds pick up and the rains fall heavily, fearing the coming of a hurricane or tropical storm. They have every right to be fretful. The last hurricane's winds reached a new high, hitting so hard that its name was retired. The hijos were too young to truly experience the last hurricane. All that your children remember is that it raged outside with their father in it. They remember that it took him away for good.

TROPICAL STORMS BECOME hurricanes when the winds pick up. But the power of the storm, the strength of it, is represented by a central pressure reading instead of wind speed even though it is the winds that are terrible, deadly. The winds picked up and uprooted the banana tree that crushed your husband's limbs beneath its trunk and buried his face under its wet, soggy leaves.

Hurricanes know who they want.

You could not get the last one to take you. You stood outside for hours, getting drenched. Raindrops fell with a forcefulness you could not describe. The storm within you was more frightening. It raged, picking up speed and swirling uncontrollably, pressing hard against your ribs, plummeting down to your stomach only to rise again and again. The beads of water slapped and pelted you, but the winds would not pick up around you and the stubborn trees clung to their muddy roots, uncooperative. When you finally dragged yourself back into the house, back to your hijos, you felt as if you had been in a fight and lost. So you decided to wait for the next hurricane. They come every five or six years, so by then the children would be old enough to take care of themselves.

The last hurricane knocked the power out of all the generators. With the children, you waited in line for over three hours for a block of ice. You carried your ice around the corner where the boys raised their guns to your head and took your block of ice away, the same as they had done to the people who had been in front of you, the same as they planned to do to the people coming after you. Nothing personal. Later—if you have the money—you can buy it back.

So when your relatives on the mainland—in New Haven, Hartford, Philadelphia, Newark, and New York—call to tell you that they have been watching the latest reports and say that the tropical storm is growing and it looks like it will be a big one and ask you how you are doing, you say, "Estoy bien."

This is the answer you give because they really don't care and they don't know anything about being a Puerto Rican in Puerto Rico anymore. When it is too cold on the mainland, they take paid vacations to fly over. They spend their money in the mall in Isla Verdes, buying clothing that is too tight for them, buying makeup that is now too dark for their wintry-pale Americano faces. They ask you to go to the cine with them and you sit there in the theater in San Juan, watching movies in English with Spanish subtitles, wondering if the very irony of the situation escapes them, sure that it does. You and your hijos give up your beds to your relatives who sleep blissfully, full of the pasteles, empanadas, and morcilla they have begged you to prepare. They eat your mangoes and papayas as though they are going out of style, excusing themselves by reminding you that mangoes are so cheap here, that they often have to pay almost two dollars for one back at home (home is what they now call the mainland) that is half as sweet. The hurricanes and tropical storms can wipe the mangoes out for seasons at a time so that they become as rare as the coquí and there aren't any to be had by anyone except by the turistas, and you sometimes have to pay much more than two dollars for one.

That is not what your relatives want to hear.

You have become a postcard to them. Beaches and good food, exotic fruit and salsa clubs; they are no better than the turistas. But you can't tell them so because they are familia.

WHEN IT IS time for them to leave, you take them to the airport, proud that it is really in Carolina even though it is listed as being in San Juan. They don't allow family members inside or anyone who is not getting on the flight. You cannot walk your relatives to their gate. You drop them off at the curb. As you drive away, you catch your hijos' eyes in the rearview mirror. You hold their gazes and drop your voice to a whisper. You point at your relatives' retreating backs and warn your hijos not to ever become like them. You tell them that if they do, a hurricane will come and sweep them away and they will end up like their father.

Palabras

THE LAST LETTER from my grandfather, Papi, to my father went
like this:

My dear son,
We are hoping this letter finds you well and happy. Alas, mi hijo,
your poor dear mother and myself are not happy at all without
you. My son, we wait eagerly for your return. We are getting
older with each day, and it would please me greatly to pass this
business from old hands like mine into strong able ones like
yours. And Esteban, he misses you. We cannot console him in
the way that only a father can. You have not laid eyes on each
other in the last six years. He will soon be nine years old. Do you
not wish to see one who is the mirror image of the boy I once
knew in you? Soon your mother and I will be too old to care
for him properly. Come back to us, my son. We are waiting to
welcome you.
Love,
your father

We are waiting to find out what my father will do—marry an island girl or come back to us. My father's response is a postcard with a backdrop of a beach in Puerto Rico with the sun setting over it that says:

Papi,
No comprendo ingles.
tu hijo

"This is how he treats his poor father, Esteban. We are all a joke to him!" Papi says, putting the postcard on top of the cash register. He begins to wipe down the Plexiglas counter with a vengeance. "Everything we've done has always been for him."

My grandfather left Carolina, Puerto Rico, for Brooklyn, New York, to forget the life he'd led as a young man selling mango, coconut, pineapple, and cherry ices from a handcart. He says he left in order to live, to really feel alive and that in order to begin again, you have to forget the life that you have already led. My father was fourteen when they moved to East New York, Brooklyn, and opened a bodega across the street from the projects on Miller Avenue under a sky less blue than the one he'd left behind. While my grandfather was trying to forget selling ices during the summers to the turistas at the beaches of San Juan and Isla Verdes, saving to come to the mainland, my father was forgetting his family, leaving us behind.

A bell over the door tinkles to announce customers, and Papi cuts off whatever else he might have said to me. Papi's face is red. He passes me the postcard. "Go upstairs and show that to your grandmother."

I wonder if my father has ever really seen a sunset like the one on the postcard and if he will ever come for me so I can see it for myself. We never know what my father will do next. Sometimes he answers Papi's letters and paints a picture of his new life in Humacao, saying that he's living close to nature like a real jíbaro, not like a Nuyorican. Sometimes he describes the mountains or El Yunque so well it brings tears of remembrance to my grandparents' eyes. He talks about Marisela, a girl he met in Ponce and moved in with. Papi wrote to him once, complaining about my difficulty with English. My Spanish was excellent, as advanced as an adult's, but I had no patience for English and I was suffering in school as a result. My father wrote back that he was pleased my Spanish was so good and that he didn't care if I never spoke English. Then he said he would only answer Papi's letters when they were written in Spanish.

Papi's letters vary too, sometimes stern and reproving, usually florid, they read like translations. He reminds my father of his duty to us and the promises he has made. My father took an extra two years to graduate high school because of his English and, after graduating, he enlisted in the army rather than go to a college for business. They agreed my father would return and take over Papi's bodega when he finished in the army; when he finished, two years ago, he flew to Puerto Rico and stayed.

ABUELA'S FACE FALLS and she rips the postcard in two. "At least this one's not all about Marisela." She turns her back and continues washing the rice for dinner, speaking to me in Spanish. "When is he going to realize we're Americans? He wants all of the things we left behind. What does he want all these things for?" My grandmother's back is bent awkwardly over the sink as she fills the pot again with water and brings the white starchy foam brimming to the top and sloshing over. She picks through the rice, looking for imperfect grains burned on the ends and small stones. She pours the water out and begins again, slower than she was before my father left. I can hate him when I see how old he is making us with his refusal to come back.

For him Papi tried to perfect his English, and for him he dragged a wife to the mainland, a wife who, unable to learn English, had no voice with which to complain. Abuela had only the Spanish that Papi was trying to forget. It was for my father's sake that they opened this bodega, lived in an apartment above the store, accepted subway tokens in lieu of payment and broke open cigarette packs to sell loosies. All for the ingratitude of a man who did not care enough to bear the weight of love.

Abuela whispers, "Dios mio, what kind of world is it where the children ignore the wishes of their parents?" Then she turns to me.

"Esteban, go over and ask Rosa if she wants a plate tonight. I'm making arroz con pollo."

We try to feed Rosa without appearing to do so. My grandparents call her hija, *daughter.*

ROSA LIVES ON the fourth floor in the projects across the street on Miller and Pitkin. She takes longer than usual to answer the door. She opens the door but stands behind it, half-dressed in a flimsy blue robe with her legs peeking out. She smiles at me, but doesn't invite me in. "Esteban."

"'Buela's making arroz con pollo tonight."

"Ah, my favorite," she says. It's my favorite too. She looks down the hallway of her apartment and whispers something to someone, then turns back to me, blushing. "But tell her that's all right. Thank you anyway."

"Okay. See you later."

There is a word for it, but I don't know what it is in English. A word—or a string of them to describe the way I feel about Rosa. Amor. Cariñoso. I'm sure Rosa knows what it is, but I can't ask her. Rosa is a full-grown woman with a husband, a lover, and secrets. She was born on the mainland like me, a Nuyorican. English is easy for her. She's unlike any of the other women I know in our neighborhood, who are just like Abuela, who consider themselves "trying" women—women who have divided their time equally between back-breaking work, cooking, church, telenovelas, and praying for sons, husbands, or brothers who have lost their way. These women speak as little English as possible and all have ailments. They constantly visit Abuela to discuss them. Mrs. Calderon has moaning knees from scrubbing floors as a young woman, Mrs. Morales' throat rattles and she wheezes from too much smoking, and my abuela's hands are gradually becoming claws, twisted and gnarled and arthritic, cramping up on her when she tries to give herself insulin shots.

AFTER GIVING ABUELA Rosa's reply, I go up the fire escape to the roof to see who Rosa was talking to. From up here I can see the whole neighborhood, the subway and dry cleaners one block away and C-Town, the supermarket, ten blocks away in the other direction after the park, the intermediate school and the hospital. I can see the outline of Rosa's body from the fire escape. The streetlights shine right through her flimsy curtains and into her bedroom. Across the street, Rosa and Yauba are doing it.

Yauba's never come to see her in the evening before, but I know it's him. I can tell by their bodies. When it's Pedro and Rosa, they argue and fight. Pedro will grab her roughly, gripping the tops of her arms and shaking her hard before pushing her toward the bed. In the bed, Rosa will lie still while Pedro moves on top of her. But Yauba and Rosa don't move that way. I watch as she shrugs out of that robe, then takes her short nightie off, her long arms upraised as she arches her back and pulls it up over her head. I live to watch Rosa. What I wouldn't give to be the nightie that's touched her skin.

Yauba gets up from the bed to take her into his arms. They move like they're dancing, swaying and teasing as they edge toward the bed and fall onto it, wrestling and rolling like children. I can't hear the sound, but I know Rosa is laughing. Across the street, Pedro's silhouette is heading home.

WHEN I COME home from school later that week, the front of the store is closed. It's never been closed early before, and I rush upstairs, anxious. Has my father returned? Nothing short of an emergency would make Papi close early. I let myself in and call out, but no one answers me. I find my grandparents in their bedroom, sitting side by side on the edge of their bed, Papi's arms around Abuela, Abuela crying. She's holding a crumpled and bunched paper in one hand up to her mouth like a handkerchief, covering the lower portion of her face with it, moaning, "Esta casado. Esta casado," *he's married*, and I know the paper is from my father. So he really went and married Marisela and he sends a telegram to tell us; he hasn't even bothered to call. All the hope I'd had of him returning for me and taking me back is like a weight of lead inside of me dropping from my chest to my feet.

Papi notices me in the doorway then. Maybe he has tears in his eyes, maybe he motions for me to join them on the corner of the bed, I don't know. I race out of the room so as not to see.

I can't say how I'm really feeling. Part of me feels the same hurt and sadness my grandparents felt, and part of me feels something like rage that I can't name.

I race across the street and up the four flights and bang on Rosa's door knocker like the police are chasing me. I can hear Rosa running to the door. Rosa comes to the door, breathless, full of concern. "Esteban? Is something wrong? What's happened?"

I don't know what to say to her. For a moment, I forget about my problem. The left half of Rosa's face is a motley of color, shadow-black under her eye and splotchy red spreading across her cheekbone and jaw like a stain. Purplish bruises dot her arms like tight rosebuds unfurling.

There is no need to ask what's happened. I want to ask her if her face is in pain. What I say is, "Why does he put those bruises on your face?" Her left cheek is swollen as if she'd stuffed her mouth with food.

She motions for me to follow her into the kitchen, where a bowl of ice sits on the counter next to a miniature TV. Rosa shrugs and puts an ice cube wrapped in a dish towel to her cheek, wincing at the shock of cold, smiling wryly, her smile twisted beneath a mask of bruises. "Why does he do it?" She turns away, lost in thought. "Well, I guess he beats me because I see Yauba." She faces me again. "And I see Yauba because he beats me."

I can't think of an appropriate thing to say. I don't want to make her angry by cursing her husband, who I think should be thrown on the third rail in the train station. Right now, he and my father are the same person. I hate them both. So I stay silent except to say, "Que lastima," *what a shame.* I remembered Abuela saying it when she heard of the hurricanes sweeping through her hometown, uprooting palm and mango trees and knocking down power lines and making it so no one could get any hot water or ice for days. It sounds appropriate, but it's not what I want to say.

Rosa switches off the mini TV on the kitchen counter and puts the bowl of ice in the freezer. "And you? What brings you here today?"

I open my mouth to tell her and nothing comes out. I try again and start to cry.

"POBRECITO," ROSA MURMURS, kneeling down to my height and pulling me into her arms. I had expected our first embrace to have the full effect of those Roman candles they shoot at the sky out in Pitkin Park on July Fourth, but it is nothing like that. Rosa feels safe to me, like a dream made real. She's soft, her voice is the ripple of a wave and the hand that strokes my hair is the touch I'd always imagined my mother would have used had she lived to love me.

I wanted to tell her about my own mother, and that all I knew of her was that she was a morena and she was dead, not even how she died or when or if my father had even loved her or whether he would have taken us all back to Puerto Rico with him if she had lived. I wanted her to know that I couldn't remember my own father's face and that he had gone back to Puerto Rico rather than raise his son and run the store that his father had created with him in mind and now lived in Humacao and was married to a new wife. I wanted her to know that the new wife, Marisela, was from Ponce and was probably the type of woman Rosa wanted to be and hated. When my father was only living with her, he'd written Papi a letter meant to hurt, bragging about how Marisela cooked his flan and mondongo soup and arroz con pollo better than Abuela ever had and that they were thinking of having a baby, and that if they did, he would marry her because he wanted his child to have a father. I wanted to tell her about my pain, pain as real as that stain of a fist on her cheek.

"Lo odio," I whisper. *I hate him.*

Rosa hushes me. "Como no," she says. *Of course.* She knew what it was like to both hate and love the same person at the same time.

I DIDN'T EXPECT to come home and find them on the phone with my father, congratulating him on his wedding. Abuela is talking rapidly in Spanish. At the same time tears stream from her eyes and she leans on Papi to keep standing.

They won't look me in the eye while they fake the part of happy parents. Papi waves me over. "Esteban, come. It's your father; he wants to speak to you." Papi tries to smile and lie at the same time, his face twisted into a half smile, half grimace. He whispers, "Somebody had to be the adults," before he pulls the phone from Abuela and thrusts it at me.

My father's chatter runs in my ears without any pause. He keeps talking about the festivities, how big the cake was, how fresh the pasteles, how sweet the platanos, how light the flan, how pretty the bride. His voice is deep, drunk, with laughter beneath it. He laughs at his own jokes and pulls the phone from his mouth to shout occasional answers to the teasing calls for him to come back to the celebration.

It's difficult to hear him with the music up loud in the background and the shouts of laughter, the rowdy toasts. A woman starts to sing a line or two in the background, then she bursts into giggles. Oh how much fun they are having while we huddle in a tiny storefront apartment and pretend to be happy for him. My father is happy with his pregnant Marisela and high off his wedding, while my grandparents stand watching me with hope. While he brags about his pretty new wife, they are hoping he is saying Marisela will now be my mother and that he will send for me or is coming to get me himself. I know they are hoping it because that's what I'm hoping. But my father keeps talking.

I waited for him to ask how I was, how tall I had gotten, did I still like to pick the green olives out of Abuela's arroz con pollo and eat them first, what would I like him to send me for my upcoming birthday, but he doesn't say any of that.

"Mami?" My father finally notices that no one has been responding to him.

"It's me," I say.

He laughs then. "What happened to Mami? You been hiding on the phone all this time?"

"I thought you wanted to speak to me?"

"Did Papi say that? Okay, let's speak together." My father laughs, then pauses. "You want a new mami? A baby sister or brother?" My father asks, his laughter painting a picture of him, not as the uniformed man in the framed picture on our living room wall, the only child of Papi and Abuela's six that survived past the age of two, but as a spoiled boy, too weak to do anything else but what he's doing, and I realize that my grandparents know this.

There is una palabra, *a word*, for a man like my father, a word that is really offensive in Spanish but that translates pretty tamely into English and I struggle to think of it, remembering that the men who come to our store call Pedro that behind his back.

"Maybe I'll give you one of each." He laughs at his own joke and I don't want to hear it, I just want to forget him. Right now Pedro and my father are the same in my eyes and I wish I could tell him so.

"No me digas nada! Te odio!" I scream, *I don't want to hear it*, and slam the phone down. My grandparents cry out as one, "Que hiciste?" *What did you do*, and they can't understand.

"Déjame en paz!" I scream, *leave me alone*, and run past them and head for the fire escape. I run up the fire escape, making my way over broken glass and loose paper.

My grandfather comes shuffling behind me, out of breath. He grabs my arm and pulls me down a few stairs until we are facing each other. I know he'll beat me now for my disrespect, but I don't care. "How dare you! Nobody raised you that way, to speak to your father so!"

He smacks me and shakes me. "You shame me! You're going to call him and say you're sorry. Then my belt's going to give you what you deserve!"

"I'm not telling him anything!" I sob, crying. I try to pull away, but Papi hugs me to him, his chin on top of my head, "Ay, niño, how could you?" My grandfather doesn't even realize he's letting us speak in Spanish.

I pull away, running up the fire escape up to the rooftop. "I hate him!" I shout.

"Come down from there!"

"I hate him! I hate him!"

At the rooftop, I can see better into Rosa's window. In the middle of my anger, I watch her and Pedro, Rosa's body lying still underneath his, Pedro on top of her, moving to his own rhythm unconcerned with anyone but himself. I hate him too. I search for a word to tell them all.

"Cabron!" I shout at their window. Papi gasps for breath on the fire-escape steps behind me. He taught me to never say that word. It means different things to different men. Men from other islands use it lightly, treat it like a nickname, but it is a hateful word where we are from, a word Papi says should never be said out loud. But that's the word I want. That's my father, and no threat of a belt is going to take it from me.

"Cabron!" I shout it again, hoping Rosa and Pedro can hear it.

"Cabron," I say it one last time for my father, wishing we were on the phone or face to face. I scream it. To me, it sounds like a raw cry in the night air, but it's really a tiny sound swallowed and absorbed by the revving engines, screeching tires, arguments over games of Cee-lo, music from boom boxes, ringing pay phones, ambulance sirens, jingling beepers, the wails of squad cars and glass breaking that make up the sounds of a night on my street.

IN THE PRAIRIE SCHOONER
BOOK PRIZE IN FICTION SERIES

To order or obtain more information on
these or other University of Nebraska
Press titles, visit nebraskapress.unl.edu.

CPSIA information can be obtained at www.ICGtesting.com
Printed in the USA
LVOW11s0650051014

407293LV00001B/12/P

9 780803 255395